GIRLS
WHO SCORE
HOT LESBIAN EROTICA

EDITED BY
ILY GOYANES

CLEiS
PRESS

Published in the United States by Cleis Press, Inc., 2246 Sixth Street, Berkeley, California 94710.

Printed in the United States.
Cover design: Scott Idleman/Blink
Cover photograph: John Fedele/Getty Images
Text design: Frank Wiedemann

First Edition.
10 9 8 7 6 5 4 3 2 1

Trade paper ISBN: 978-1-57344-825-3
E-book ISBN: 978-1-57344-839-0

Contents

INTRODUCTION

P ossessing an intimate knowledge of what makes writers tick
(being one myself), I shouldn't have been caught off guard
when the submissions for this anthology started coming in. See,
when the idea for *Girls Who Score* was first conceived, its muse
was not an ethereal, willowy goddess with a name like Poly-
hymnia or Terpsichore, but she was a goddess all the same: the
very traditional (and some might say very cliché) sporty dyke.

You may call her by another name, but in my city, in my
social circles, that is what she is commonly referred to as. And
although the moniker you have applied to her kind may differ,
you know her just as well as I do. She was the catcher on your
high school's softball team—the one you would catch staring
at you with a shy smile in your second-period biology class.
She was the tall, tough basketball player who strutted her way
through your college campus—the one whose shorts seemed
always about to fall off—and oh, how you wished they would.
The long and lean track star, the short and muscular soccer
player—their silhouettes are what ran through my head like

so many ESPN clips as I thought, *The sporty dyke deserves some credit.*

Because, in real life, she rarely gets the credit she deserves. I hear some WNBA teams are still around, but in my hometown, the Sol only lasted about as long as a relationship built on a one-night stand. And although some professional female competitors, such as Olympic athletes and professional golfers, have the option of a career, my *cliché* girls, my *traditional* girls, could never make a living playing a sport such as football, basketball or baseball. In fact, women aren't even supposed to play baseball—they play *soft*ball.

Even though they may not get a lot of action on the field after high school and college, they always manage to see a lot of action off the field. Because female athletes have an easy confidence about them, a natural nonchalance and usually a killer bod that draws all kinds of women to them—straight, lesbian, bisexual, curious, questioning, you name it.

Alas, as I delved into the nature (and killer bod) of the sporty dyke, I somehow managed to get lost in my thoughts. What was I talking about? Oh yes, *writers.* As I was saying, when I started receiving stories about yoga instructors and roller derby enthusiasts, I shouldn't have been surprised. Women are competitive by nature, whether they play *sports* or *games.* Women play hard and love harder. They don't just score—they keep track. So as I read story after story of complex, intriguing women engaging in all kinds of, ahem, contact sports, I realized that girls who score aren't always playing ball, so to speak. After all, scuba divers and gym bunnies *are* in fact athletes, and writers are very... creative. Yes—creative and inspiring.

So inspiring in fact, that "Lucky Number Three," Beth Wylde's story about a hockey player who gives her all during the championship game—both on the ice and in the locker room—

reminded me of the fact that women even played hockey (I chalk my lapse in memory up to the fact that I live in a tropical climate where hockey is just an afterthought).

Sinclair Sexsmith, who has forever redefined the term *gym bunny* for me, knocked my calf-length tube socks off with "A Good Workout." Not only does the story involve a pairing that I find both rare and almost unbearably hot, but the description of their "workout" lingers long after you turn the last page.

"Give and Go," by Anna Watson, really hits home with its realism. I have always been fond of Watson's work, but this story particularly touched me because I can sympathize with the main character about how hard it is to find the time to fuck your wife between running errands, running children and running away from deadlines (be they work or otherwise). "Give and Go" also touches on the sobering (and titillating) reality of being a lone dyke in a locker room full of naked, "straight" girls.

The characters in Kiki DeLovely's story, "Facing the Music," don't have to worry about kids, chores or any of that mundane nonsense. They can (and do) get it on just about anytime, anywhere. JT Langdon's "Boot Camp" reminds us that a little motivation goes a long way, and the characters in Delilah Devlin's "Playing the Field" are so devilishly endearing that I wish I could call upon some Disney magic to turn them into real live girls.

"Hail Mary," by Shanna Germain, resonates with me because it serves as the standard by which all "serious" erotica should be judged. Erotica can take many forms, from the purely entertaining fluff piece designed to push you over the edge, to the poignant literary masterpiece that also contains some smoldering sex scenes. The only common denominator is (or should be) eroticism. There needs to be some sweet sex, some scandalous sexual tension—*something* sexy *somewhere* in the story.

And although I love whimsical, entertaining erotica, I get an electrical charge out of reading a *really great story that happens to have sex in it*. "Hail Mary" is that story.

Although some of the stories in this anthology are not what I was expecting when I started on this journey, they're all stories that alternately moved me or made me laugh. And perhaps more importantly, they all made me feel the need to "hit the showers."

ily goyanes
Miami, Florida

CHAIRS

Sommer Marsden

W hat's the problem, Bowmen?" Chevy darted to my left and intercepted the basketball like a bear plucking a salmon from a river. She moved like some sleek and predatory animal.

I moved like I had concrete blocks strapped to my feet.

This is what happens when you like your phys ed instructor and actually listen to her *natural talent* speech, and her insistence that even in college, *extracurricular* looks good on your record.

"Nothing," I mutter and move back and out of the way of the very aggressive girl from the opposing team.

"Hustle," Chevy shouts, and then she's moving. Toward our basket, toward a score. Away from me.

My legs feel like Jell-O and soft bread, but I run anyway. At least I can *look* like I know what I'm doing.

I hate basketball, have I said?

* * *

"You need to get on the ball out there, Bowmen. So to speak."
Chevy laughs at her own joke and winks.

My insides turn to warm goo and dirty thoughts. "Sorry,"
I mutter.

The remainder of the team is showered and filing out of the
locker room. I don't know where Chevy's gone, but after the
game—the one that we barely won and only thanks to her—I
find myself a big, cold soda; sit on the cool, stained tile floor and
drink it slowly while my skin cools.

"You need to strengthen up those thigh muscles. You move
like a marionette with only half her strings." She pulls her long
yellow hair from a band, and her eyes—gray like the ocean
before a storm—settle on me. "You know, tighten up."

I nod, my tongue a useless thing lying in my mouth. I can
never speak to her when I look directly at her. She makes all of
me tremble with a bizarre mix of want and anticipation.

She cocks her head. "Are you listening?"

"Y-yes," I say.

"I can help you."

Now, I'm curious. And terrified. Chevy—short for Chevron—
is not the kind to take excuses or extend pity. If she helps me it
will be by bending me to her will. And when that thought crosses
my mind, my nipples grow hard inside my sweaty team shirt.

She takes three big steps toward me and without thinking, I
press my back to the lockers. I can't seem to breathe, and I'd give
my right arm for a long hot shower before she gets too close.
Surely I smell. Somehow she never does—at least not to me—
she just always smells like Chevy. Cotton, a little sweat, coconut
shampoo and rubber from her tennis shoes.

"Would you like that, Bowmen?" she asks, brushing a lock
of my sweaty brown hair off my shoulder.

She is the only person in the world who calls me Bowmen instead of Andrea or Andi. But I let her because it's like a secret nickname. Just one that everyone hears her use.

"Sure," I wheeze, and she laughs. It's more of a dark chuckle, but she nods, removes her shirt with a one-handed, over-the-head grab and tosses it in the hamper. "Shower up. Lesson one in ten."

And then she's gone into the cavernous echoing room that is shower room one. I strip and hurry into shower room two, hoping that no one is in there, hoping that I can just catch my breath. And think. And breathe.

It only seems like I have time enough to wash my hair before I hear Chevy yelling, "Well? Are you coming or what, Bowmen?"

I squeeze out my hair and wrap myself in the towel that is more like a washcloth. "Sorry, I must have lost track of time and I—" I move to rush past her but she clotheslines me. Not hard enough to hurt me, just hard enough that I bounce back and slow down.

"Where you going so fast, Andi?"

When she calls me Andi a slow, warm slide of fluid issues from me. I blush because I have no panties on to impede its progress. I have nothing to cover me but a school-issued towel that could be a tea towel for all of its ability to conceal.

"To get dressed?"

I hold my breath, listen. We are alone here. The only ones who remain after the game. This both terrifies and thrills me.

"Nah. I think we're good. This won't take long. Your legs are weak. I'll show you how to do chairs."

Chairs? That doesn't sound so bad.

"Some people call them wall squats, but because of my golden rule for thigh strengthening, we'll call them chairs."

"Why?" I manage, as she pushes me to a section of pale

yellow cinder-block wall. She pushes her hands down hard on my shoulders so that I have to sink down the wall. Slowly.

"Because you're going to do your best impression of a chair. It should be such an uncanny resemblance that I am tempted to sit in your lap." She winks at me and there is another warm rush between my legs.

I want to moan, both from arousal and embarrassment, but I bite my lip instead.

I am now pressed against the wall, towel slipping, doing my best impression of a chair.

"Nice," Chevy says and I feel a stupid rush of gratitude for her approval. "Feel it in your legs?"

I nod.

"Your core?" she asked, touching my belly through the towel. The muscles there seem to jump and kick at her touch. I suck in a shaky breath.

I nod.

"Good. Now hold it for a minute."

A minute!

"Yes, a minute," she chuckles, reading my mind.

I watch the anorexic second hand sweep the standard-issue clock and when the final fifteen seconds starts to rush toward me, Chevy leans on my trembling thighs with her forearms and presses down.

I make a noise like some dying thing and she grins at me, white teeth flashing in the fluorescent lighting.

"You can do it, Bowmen. Five more seconds."

My legs are truly shaking now. No fine quiver here; a bone-deep shaking has taken its place. "I can't."

"Two," she says, "and there's a reward."

A reward?

Her eyes stay on the clock and when she turns to me and

laughs, I start to straighten up.

"Wait," she says.

Her mouth is hot and soft when it closes down on mine. Her lips just as demanding as the rest of her. My breath stills in my lungs, my heart erupts in a chaotic new rhythm and then Chevy slips a finger into my pussy, curls it hard against my smooth inner walls and a flexing kind of shiver works through me.

"Good girl," she says, curling that finger one more time. And then she stands, leaving me sagging there. "I'll see you tomorrow. We'll practice some more."

And then she's gone.

"Ready? You were better out there today."

Practice had been a mind fuck. Me trying to move fast and eager and somewhat gracefully all the while thinking of Chevy's finger in my pussy and her lips on my mouth. I had found myself blushing more than once and several times running fast just to clear my head. She'd taken it for improvement.

Talk about blind luck.

"I tried."

Everyone is gone; it's just us. I have showered and judging by her wet hair, so has she. My eyes are greedy and I can't help but track a drop of water that runs from her collarbone down inside her white cotton tank to nestle between her breasts.

"You did good. Now do better. Go lower this time."

I press my body to the wall, my towel yet to be replaced by clothes. I blame myself and, yes, a secret urge to be alone with her mostly naked. I sink down into a chair position and try to focus on anything that isn't the pain in my legs. I've wanted Chevy since the first time she shouted, "Heads up, girly! You daydreaming or what?"

Ever since then, I've been daydreaming about *her*.

"Lower, Bowmen," she says, leaning in, her hot breath feathering over my face and in my hair. Excitement and a tiny bite of fear works through my gut, and I do as she says.

"One minute starts now," Chevy says. And she does it again, waits till the very end and bears down on me with her forearms until my body starts to shake and my inner thighs feel like rubber bands that have been stretched too far.

I literally sob when that minute is ticked off and she leans in, pushes her hands into my wet hair and kisses me. Her tongue tastes minty like toothpaste as she strokes it over mine. When Chevy breaks the kiss she knocks my towel away and runs a finger over the flat of my belly. Her other fingers capture my nipple and pinch. I gasp and a wet flexing starts deep in my cunt. One more kiss, and Chevy says, "Again. Go lower."

"Lower?" I gasp, but I sink back down in chair position when she pushes my shoulders.

"Yes, lower."

I hold my breath without realizing it as my legs begin to shake almost immediately. In the bowels of the athletic department, I hear the floor waxer kick on. What if we're discovered? What if someone from janitorial comes in? What if...

"Concentrate, Bowmen," Chevy snaps.

"Sorry. I can't."

"You can."

She pushes her fingertips against my trembling stomach and says, "Just block everything out. You're stronger than you think. And in the end...in the end, you'll be glad you did it."

I wait for that minute to drag by, a silent dirge made of slow-moving seconds. Finally, she says, "Good. Done."

When I start to stand up to give my screaming muscles a rest, she forces two slim, cool fingers inside of me and I feel an orgasm creeping close—the first tentative spasms of release.

"God, Chevy. Please," I whisper, bolder than I've ever been with her.

"Again," she says, grinning. "Deeper bend this time."

I gape at her. Is she kidding? Is she insane? There is *no* way.

But I bow my head and flex my thighs and inch my back down the pale yellow wall so that I am a chair. A deep-seated chair, sitting lower than I have before. When Chevy drops to her knees in from of me and forces my thighs apart, so I am a *splayed* chair, I want to cry. Both from excitement and pain. There is no way I can stay this way for a second, let alone a minute, but if she's about to do what I think she's going to do, an earthquake couldn't move me.

"Stay," she commands, serious gray eyes flashing.

My thighs start to quake immediately, but my heart is in danger of failing me because she leans forward, tongue out, and presses the wet tip—and only the tip—to my clit. I almost come. But my body is so tortured, I can't quite get there.

Chevy starts small, rigid circles on that swollen bit of flesh and my fingers clench around nothing. Just air. I can't even bear the thought of putting my hands on my thighs, that tiny bit of extra pressure would be too much.

She circles, circles, circles with her tongue until I think I might scream. And still the clock ticks by so, so slowly.

"Shh," she says, when I make some desperate noise. "Almost done."

The minute is gone, eaten by pain. I drop without grace or pretense to the floor where my discarded towel lies.

Then Chevy has prostrated herself before me as if she's praying. She's on her knees, bent forward, head down, and she is licking me. Her tongue is sweet and hot and so, so welcome. She sucks my clit and licks me harder with her broad flattened tongue. She shoves her fingers deep into my weeping cunt and starts to fuck me in earnest.

"Oh, good. So, so good." I'm shivering and shaking and want to cry it feels so good.

"You did good. The more you do, the stronger you'll be. The stronger you are, the more confident your game."

It's almost conversational, her running monologue. She pauses to kiss the insides of my thighs and lick my mound. She rears up and kisses me full on the lips so I can taste my own juices on her perfect mouth. Her fingers don't stop and she thrusts harder, curling them aggressively. Then she bends forward, returns her tongue and sucks my clit with enough force that I cry out.

And then I'm coming. That damned waxer humming lowly somewhere in the gym. The most bad-ass girl on the team practically on her belly sucking me off. A fine tremble still shaking my exhausted thighs. That's when I start to laugh.

"Good for you, Bowmen. A sense of humor will get you places," Chevy says, sitting up. She palms my breasts and kisses me one more time. "Now come on."

I take her hand as she stands and offers it. She pulls me to my feet and I wait for my heart to stop pounding and my legs to stop shaking. "Where're we going?"

"Food and then..." She winks.

"And then?"

"More chairs. You didn't think I was done with you, did you? You have tons more to do before your thighs are as strong as I want them."

"Oh?"

"But don't worry. I'll make it worth your while."

I just bet she will. But I plan to make it worth her while too. Every good trainer deserves her own reward.

BLOOD LUST

Gina Marie

R ae knew the minute she saw the chick's blood on her face
that she had to have her. What was her name?

"Fuck you, bitch—I'm taking you out!" were the only words
she heard the cunt say. What did her coach call her? Marinda?
Even though it was just a sparring match, girls always fight to
kill. Marinda was no exception, and she fought like an animal.
Rae guessed she fucked like one too. In the locker room, Rae
pulled her hair out of the rubber band, letting the thick waves
loose, and tipped her chin up into the mirror to examine the
damage.

That's when she saw it, a little smear of the bitch's dark
blood; a long, thick streak at the edge of the bruise staining her
right cheek purple. The sight of it made her incredibly hot.

Of course, it didn't take much. Rae had been horny since she
had discovered a dirty magazine in her grandfather's nightstand
drawer when she was fourteen. She'd never forgotten the story
of hot lesbians exploring the wild side—words like *juice* and

tight turning her on even then. If she had been a good girl, she would have stuffed that rag right back where she found it, but she wasn't and she didn't. She'd crouched in the semidark of the bedroom and flipped it open to a hot tale of lesbian lust and a few other surprises.

By the time she heard footsteps and was forced to put the magazine back in its not-so-hidden hiding place, all of those delicious words had been seared into her brain. Fuck. Cherry. Dildo. Slick. Cock. Hard. Tit. Pop. Blow. Red. Cunt. Down. Dong. Bang. Spread. Wet. Hard. Pinch. Stroke. She spent the entire afternoon whispering them to herself, enjoying the way they felt in her mouth, the way they buzzed in her brain, the wicked way they tingled everywhere else.

She whispered the words now as she thought about Marinda—tangling with her in the sheets, biting at her bruised skin, strapping on a huge black dildo and slamming it into Marinda's shiny red cunt. She could taste the salty sweetness of Marinda's knife-point nipples, hear the pussy-wrenching stream of filthy words spewing from her naughty mouth.

Rae felt her clit harden as she closed her eyes and played the sparring match back in her mind, remembering the Christmas-y feeling of joy that comes with a good, solid blow to the face... the sexual excitement of striking Marinda's jaw hard, the thrill of watching the little trickle of blood from her cut lip streaming down her chin.

Rae stood there lost in lust-thought in front of the mirror, a wet towel poised to wipe the blood away. At that moment Marinda walked in and stood behind her, staring her reflection down, her jaw puffy, eyes flashing with anger, her face still glazed with a bright sheen of sweat.

Rae put the towel down and straightened her back. "Nice fight, bitch."

"You too, whore."

Marinda moved in close and grabbed Rae's ass, not once removing her dark, vicious gaze from Rae's reflection in the mirror.

"I know what you want from me, Sugar Rae."

"Oh, yeah?"

"Yeah, I've been around."

"Don't fuck with me, Marinda."

"It's Lucinda to you, Miss Cherry pie à la fucking mode."

"Fine. Don't fuck with me, Lucinda."

"Oh, I will fuck with you. I will fuck with you till you can't take it anymore. But you won't get it that easy."

"Really? Is that your game? Playing hard to get?"

Rae was breathing hard; Marinda's hands were reaching around, her fingers teasing Rae's crotch.

"No, baby, not hard to get. Hard to hit. Best two out of three."

Rae nearly exploded on the spot. She wiped the blood from her cheek and turned around. Lucinda leaned forward and pulled Rae in close by the back of her neck, their lips nearly touching.

"Bring your best game, lover girl," she growled. "I don't know what's going on in your twisted fucking mind, but just so *you* know, if you lose—and you most likely will—you'll be begging for mercy at the working end of my whip."

Rae licked her lower lip and smiled seductively. "You toss me a cherry bomb and I'll throw you a grenade. I'm always ready for action. May the best bitch win."

Lucinda's manager arranged a three-fight matchup and promoted the hell out of it. Posters, radio announcements, media coverage—the works. The bawdy crowd of spectators may have felt a certain "sexlectric" charge in the air, but of course they didn't know what the true stakes were. The personal challenge wasn't announced in the paper.

After two draws, Lucinda nailed Rae on the last night with a blow that put her on her ass and nearly knocked her out. She got back up in time, but couldn't find her rhythm. A deal's a deal. Time to pay up.

In the locker room after the final match, Rae did her best to ignore Lucinda as she stripped out of her gear and sweat-drenched clothing with an air of winner's bravado. Then Rae felt a tap on her shoulder and turned around slowly. Lucinda stood inches away, naked, the smell of battle rising from her skin. Her eyes flashed fire. She handed Rae a slip of paper: *You lose. 540-555-0990.*

Rae imagined Lucinda laced up tight in a black vinyl corset and crotchless panties, standing over her as she awaited punishment on all fours, collared and leashed like a tamed beast. She could see, could hear, the lashing sound as Lucinda gripped the leather handle and cocked her muscular arm. She could feel her ass stinging as she took her loser's place at the working end of the whip. She preferred to be the girl on top, but the dirty thoughts still caused her pussy to scream and drip, hot thick juice sliding down her thighs. And those words, those dangerous words, came swirling back into her mind. Fuck. Crop. Slip. Core. Hard. Bite. Knife. Whip. Growl. Slide. Clit. Ache.

Without a word and without looking up, Rae took the number from Lucinda's taped fingers, tucked it into the pocket of her gym bag and continued toweling off.

Saturday evening, Rae pushed the numbers into her cell. Lucinda answered on the sixth ring. "Lucy here."

"Hi Lucinda, uh, Lucy, it's Rae. You know, the loser."

"Loser Rae! Hello, baby!"

Lucinda sounded almost sweet on the phone. Rae was a bit taken aback, unsure of how to respond to her tone.

"So, uh, what do you...?"

Lucinda rattled off an address on the east side of town. "See you at my place at five."

When Rae pulled up in her car, Lucinda was sitting on the curb in front of a row of loft apartments and shops, licking at pink drippings sliding down the side of a double-scoop strawberry ice-cream cone. She was quite innocent looking in a green and white polka dot shirtdress and strappy sandals. Her hair hung loose and shiny, her lips tinted dark red and wet with sugar and cream.

What about rage? What about punishment?

Lucinda waved, licked and smiled.

"Hey, babe! Welcome to the 'hood! That's my loft up there—with the black balcony rail. Want a cone? Moxy's makes the best ice cream in the universe. Hand cranked and triple whipped!"

Forget about the cone—Rae would be happy to lick the drips right from Lucinda's hot lips.

"I'd love a cone," Rae smiled.

As she stood at the counter ordering, Rae glanced back at Lucinda, still sitting on the curb mouthing her treat.

Rae carried her hand-cranked, triple-whipped cone outside and lapped at the cool creaminess with the tip of her tongue.

Lucinda stood and smoothed her dress, then leaned toward Rae. "You have some ice cream on your..." She smiled, leaned closer and slowly licked the drip from Rae's cheek.

A jumble of words began popping through Rae's brain again.

Silky. Candy. Softly. Lusty. Drippy. Sweetly. Horny. Sexy. Smoothly. Slippery. Fuck.

Maybe losing wasn't so bad after all.

Rae followed Lucy upstairs into her loft. She licked her cone and looked around. The place was gorgeous—sparely yet beautifully furnished, the walls painted in the soothing colors of earth and basalt—Rae thought it looked like a Zen love palace. The minimalist décor gave the space a sense of elegance without being "soft." Rae felt herself moisten as Lucy took her on a quick tour. *Fuck shui,* she thought to herself as she took it all in. Gorgeous black-and-white photography hung in gallery frames. Cityscapes were interspersed with nudes and shots of simple objects like rocks and water.

"Lucy, your place is beautiful. Are you a photographer?"

Lucy turned and stole a mouthful of Rae's cone, smacking her lips, ignoring the question. "The master bedroom is this way."

A king-sized futon covered with a dark gray silk comforter and white silk pillows embroidered with Asian cranes was situated slightly off center, set off by a wall-mounted headboard made of hundreds of small, glossy river stones. There was nothing else in the room except professionally framed photographs similar to the ones hanging throughout the loft, a simple walnut dresser, a woven bamboo lamp and an antique black lacquer chair. As they entered what seemed like a sacred space, Lucy lifted a large black professional-looking digital camera from the dresser.

"Yes, I am a photographer—my other job when I'm not beating the shit out of people. Smile and look pretty."

Rae began tumbling through a hot naked photo shoot in her mind as Lucy simply tilted the camera slightly and clicked once.

"You fill the frame nicely," Lucy smiled, clicking again, the camera now level with Rae's torso, casually held in Lucy's hands.

"That's so cool," Rae said sincerely. "These must be your photographs on the walls. They're amazing. I have the most

unglamorous job in the world—when I'm not beating the shit
out of people, of course. I own a small landscaping business."

"Landscaping is totally artistic," Lucy said, raising the
camera again, snapping a few candid shots. "But enough about
what you do. Let's see what you've got."

Rae almost blushed before she went with Lucy's cue.

"You did kick my ass. I guess I have to obey."

Rae lifted her shirt to show off her navel. "You got me good
right here," she said, pointing to a fading bruise low on her
torso near her right hip.

"You are so ripped," Lucy said, enjoying the peek at Rae's
bare skin. "I remember that one—I could feel my fist bouncing
off of your abs—like bones tapping on a kettle drum. Now take
off your shirt, loser," she commanded, still looking so fucking
cute in her polka dots.

Rae smiled and slowly began lifting her top—a black halter
with a gathered bust and orange poppies blooming up the side.

Her unencumbered breasts blossomed forth as she pulled
the cotton fabric over her head and stood there defiantly, Lucy
circling around as if warming up for a sparring match, pressing
the shutter again and again.

"Nice *tatas, chica!*" Lucy exclaimed. "Damn!"

"Thank you for the compliment, Lucinda," Rae said in a
snarky voice, her pussy dying for attention. She wanted to grab
Lucy and take her down to the floor, but she just stood there
obediently, completing Lucy's fuck shui décor, bare breasted
and barefoot in faded, tight blue jeans.

Lucy set the camera down and moved in close, wrapping her
arms tightly around Rae's waist.

"You smell good too. You smell like...mm...like some kind
of berry."

"Berry? I smell like a berry?"

"Not any berry—some kind of berry, but I can't place it. Something unusual, but familiar. You smell fresh."

Lucy tilted her head, her glossy hair sweeping across Rae's arm, driving her crazy with lust. Lips parted slightly, she kissed Rae firmly but tenderly full on the mouth, then opened her lips a little more and tickled Rae's lips with the soft tip of her tongue.

Finally tasting her was like quenching a terrible thirst. Rae kissed her back, accepting Lucy's open invitation. The women pressed together, their lean, muscular bodies forming a statuesque pillar in the center of the room.

"Do I *taste* like an unusual berry?" Rae questioned as Lucy began sucking on one of her breasts, her other hand reaching around to her ass.

"You taste like sin. Delicious, hot sin."

Rae ran her hands through Lucy's hair and leaned back as Lucy continued to pleasure her nipples and breasts, pressing them together and biting lightly, her tongue smooth and soft.

Suddenly, she stopped and pulled away.

Rae tried to pull her back.

"Not yet. Get dressed. We're going on a picnic."

"We are?"

Rae wanted to fuck. Here. Now. In the fuck shui shrine. God, she wanted it bad. A picnic?

"I want you to feed me grapes and read poetry to me. I warned you that you'd be at the working end of my whip, remember?"

Fuck! Rae sighed with resignation and pulled her shirt back on, slowly tying it back into place before fetching her shoes and purse. Lucy changed into sexy jean short-shorts and a plain white V-neck T-shirt.

In the kitchen, Lucy pulled a bottle of wine and some food containers from the refrigerator. She placed them in a quaint little wicker basket and handed Rae a woven blanket.

"My car's around back."

Rae's nipples tingled and her cunt throbbed as they hopped into Lucy's silver convertible Maserati.

"It's definitely picnic weather," Rae said, trying to sound accommodating.

"Yes, and the water will be perfect."

Lucy pulled on her shades and turned to Rae, grinning as they sped off.

"What water?"

"Athens Lake. You ever been there?"

"I've done some bike riding around there—it's nice."

"I know of a secret little place where we can hang out and go for a swim."

"I didn't bring a suit."

"You don't need a suit in the dark."

They arrived at the lake and Rae followed Lucy like an obedient servant loaded down with picnic supplies, down a trail that opened up onto a secluded grassy shore that sloped to the water. A few fishermen, tiny specks on the opposite bank, were the only people around.

"Very nice!" Rae said with all sincerity, folding out the blanket. "This is such a great spot."

Lucy lay down on the blanket and tilted her face to catch the last few rays of the sun. "What a beautiful evening."

Rae began unpacking the basket, laying out Lucy's meticulously prepared meal—cheese, olives, French bread, seedless black grapes, cherries, a plate of crudités, the bottle of red wine, and a dense-looking chocolate truffle cake with raspberry sauce.

"Grapes milady, as you requested."

Rae held a juicy grape in her mouth and leaned over Lucy, slowly sliding it between her lips as the sun sank lower and lower on the horizon. Pretty soon they had polished off everything but the cake, including the entire bottle of wine.

"Just leave your clothes on the blanket. Come on!"

Lucy was serious about swimming. The sun had long since set. Stars had begun blinking on across the sky, reflecting in the inky blackness of the lake.

Rae held out her hand and let Lucy pull her into the water, the initial shock sending shivers up her legs and across her butt. Silt and small stones on the lake bottom felt good on the soles of her feet.

The starlight words began to rise. Fuck. Dark. Mouth. Wave. Cool. Star. Kiss. Skin. Stone. Glide. Sky. Float.

The three-quarter moon cast a silver net across the water. Lucy pulled Rae deeper until they were both nipple high in the water, their hair floating atop the ripples.

Rae pulled Lucy's slippery naked body into hers, sliding her hand between her legs, finally connecting with her sex, the heat of her pussy radiating through the coolness of the water, warming Rae's fingers.

"Kiss me there," Lucy whispered.

Rae slid under the water and held onto Lucy's hips as she sought her heat with her tongue. She licked at her softness, pressing her cheeks into Lucy's goose-pimpled thighs for as long as she could before coming up for air.

"My turn."

Lucy dove down to return the favor. Rae leaned her head back to soak in the seduction of the night sky, little wavelets and ripples forming around them as they stirred the blackness with their bodies.

God, Lucy's tongue on her clit was like a gift. She came up for air and Rae dove onto her breasts, sliding her hands around their perfect form, letting them float into her mouth. She continued to tease Lucy's breasts, then lifted her ass and tilted her back until she was floating. Rae held Lucy's weightless body on the surface of the water and slid her fingers deep into her cunt. Rae fucked her harder as she felt Lucy's lips swell with pleasure.

Lucy's long legs spread wide in the water as she floated. The only sounds were intermittent frogs and crickets, a light breeze blowing through the surrounding trees and the lapping of wavelets across their skin. Lucy's face shone silver in the moonlight. She tilted her head back farther in the water as Rae fucked her, rubbing her clit with her thumb, her fingers sinking deeper and deeper into her cunt, lifting her hips higher in the water. Lucy let out a constricted breath and her muscles clenched. Rae watched her face intently, entranced by Lucy's eyelids and cheekbones glowing in the moonlight, her mouth open, tongue out slightly and gliding across her upper lip as she shuddered. "Yesss. Oh, sweet Sugar Rae, yesss."

Rae couldn't take her eyes off of Lucy as she came, the look of pleasure on her face so intensely powerful. It was that same Christmas-y feeling as a solid blow to the jaw, except better. It was so much better. It was Christmas and the Fourth of July all at once. All fireworks and snow, every celebration, every joy, all wrapped up in one fantastic moment.

Lucy slowly returned to consciousness, let her body drop back into the blackness and pulled Rae close, wrapping herself around her.

"Rae, you fuck like an animal," she moaned, kissing Rae's ears and neck and throat.

"That's what I saw in you when we sparred that day, and when I walked into the locker room and saw your blood on my face, it was like a beast had been unleashed. I wanted to fuck you right then. I still do. I want more."

Lucy unwrapped her legs from Rae's body and bobbed in the

water. "Well, Sugar Rae, there's plenty more where that came from. Let's pack up. We forgot about dessert. How about some chocolate cake back at my place?"

Rae followed the path of silver shore, admiring Lucy's skin glowing white as her nakedness emerged from the water.

Midnight words lapped at the shore as they dried off.

Fuck. Dream. Taste. Moon. Soft. Sing. Lips. Love. Lust. Night. Good.

A GOOD WORKOUT

Sinclair Sexsmith

You check out my ass in the mirror across from mine, and that's when I know that you want me. I've got one of those too-small towels wrapped around my waist and another too-small towel draped over my shoulders, and so do you. The half-dozen girls in the locker room are wearing their towels up over their breasts, with a second one twisted up on their heads. But we don't need that. Your hair is the same length as mine, cut way above the ears, but yours has that faux-hawk, which tells me you might be a few years younger than I am. Mine I sweep up and over in a wave like I took a palm full of product and ran my hands over my head—which I did.

I wash my hands and head for the steam room, catching your eyes in the mirror for just the quickest inviting smile. I can feel the pulse in my muscles from the 5k run I just finished on the treadmill and the quick set of weights I lifted to keep my shoulders strong and open. My neck feels loose, my fingers feel heavy, my thighs feel solid.

When you chose the treadmill next to mine, I didn't think much of it. I read you as a guy for a full minute until you stopped walking and started running, and I stole a glance and noticed the smooth girl curve of your chin. Your run was lithe— supple and graceful, full of ease. I struggled with my breath and concentrated on my feet hitting the treadmill. I slowed down and caught my breath, sped up and pushed myself, slowed down again. You stayed steady, one foot in front of the other, sweating but not out of breath, listening to your iPod while I watched a rerun of "Sex and the City" on one of the flat screens.

When I left the weights to head down to the locker room, I thought I felt your eyes on me, but I didn't turn around to look. You were doing assisted pull-ups by then, your blue basketball shorts bunched by your knees as you knelt on the machine and your biceps popping. I heard you groan only once.

Not that I was watching.

And now I lay myself out on the high bench in the steam room. I'm the only one in here. I unwrap the towel and let my skin sweat the work out of me, feeling my muscles relax, the blood still pumping inside, the tingling sensation that rises after using my body. I breathe in and out, focusing on the place where my body hits the air, the place at my nasal septum where the air is leaving my body, cooler from inside my lungs than it is in the steam. I can't stay in here too long, but I love how it leaves my body supple. It feels like a cleanse, a good sweat, while working out feels like a release of toxins.

I always have the urge to run my hands over my body, feel my skin slick with sweat, open my legs and let everything get washed by the hot steamy air. I always think of that story from Nancy Friday's book *My Secret Garden* where two women in the steam room get it on—definitely a story that told me I liked what these women did together a little bit more than I expected.

I let my body sink into the tile bench and for a short minute all is still; then the door opens, releasing a gush of steam and sucking in cool air in exchange. I don't have to look up to know it's you. It seems obvious in this moment that you'd follow me in here. You sit on the bench below mine and your head is aligned with my knee. You sigh, hands on your thighs, legs parted. I can just make out your shape through the white steam. The back of your neck starts to drip. You take the towel from your shoulders and reveal your chest, small and tight and muscled, your nipples hard and pointed, rosy pink. I have the urge to reach out and twist them, feel them hard between my fingertips. I resist.

When you lean your head back and I feel your hair touch my knee, I take the hint and shift, bending my knee up over the edge of the upper bench. You sigh again, this time more of a groan, and your desire is palpable. Your eyes are closed, but you turn your head and your face is between my thighs. My heart pumps faster in my chest and my stomach rises and falls. You only wait a beat before turning your hips and gripping my inner thighs in each of your hands. You take a long inhale of the wetness that has gathered, my pubic hair thick and wet, already swelling. You take my clit in your mouth without fanfare, just slide it right in and run your tongue along the shaft. Your hands grip harder and your throat opens to take me deeper, your nose buried in my flesh. I know I must smell, musty and thick and sour, and you lap it up with your tongue, your lips pursed, shoved against me hard.

You bring one hand over to cup me underneath and I feel your fingers gently in my crack, palm against my opening, holding my lips like I have balls, high and tight and smooth. I feel your finger find my asshole and shift my body to give my consent, pushing gently against, and you slip inside, just to the first knuckle, easy with all this steam. I grip your hair, because that's what a faux-hawk is for. Long enough to grab on top and move your mouth around how I want it, where I want to feel it. I fuck your mouth while keeping your head stationary and you work your finger gently and firmly in my tight hole, your tongue wide and throat open. My hips open and I thrust into you, ready to come, thinking about shooting as my clit pulses and contracts, my body shuddering.

I pull your head back as I get supersensitive to the touch and you wipe your mouth with the back of your hand, look up at me through the steam.

I grin. I breathe and feel my feet on the floor, get my bearings and don't waste time. You are on the edge of your seat; I easily grab your waist and flip you around, your ass against me, my arms around you, one hand pushed between your legs and the other twisting those pink nipples. As my fingers find you wet and open you bring my other hand up to your mouth and suck two of them down, tongue swollen, lips wet. I keep my grip around you as I plunge two fingers inside you deep and you groan again, that same release that all those pull-ups had you uttering, the same instinct to buckle and pulse overtaking you. I pull my fingers out slick with your juices and find your clit, start jacking you off, the shaft of it hard and swollen under my fingers, throbbing with my touch.

You quicken under me.

I pull you back against me and our bodies slide against each other, your back against my large chest, my nipples still hard, my stomach against your lower back, your ass against my pelvis. If I had a cock it'd be in your ass right now, and as soon as I think that I can feel it, and you press back against me as if opening up, squirming, and I keep my grip as I reach around you to jack you off. You aren't easy to get off, I can feel it, that barrier between us, but I can feel how you like to be taken, how you like to be a boy under my touch, how you like to bend over and give it up for me, because that's how I like it, too.

Our bodies are talking to each other without our heads getting in the way. Our cocks are hard and thrusting, and I am thrusting, and you are thrusting into my palm. Your hand pushing my fingers deeper into your mouth though it is open and you're breathing around it, I feel your breath cooler than the air. My arms are dripping with sweat and steam; I can feel it rolling down my skin. You groan and I feel the vibration of your tongue on the pads of my fingers. You shudder and your back arches and I hold you up. Your other hand goes down on top of my hand between your legs and you start working it faster and faster, just a little bit up and right of where my fingers were, moving me over, until you stumble forward just a little and I feel your stomach crunch, tighten, your shoulders curl forward, your muscles shaking against me, and you come in my hand with a gush of heat and liquid.

You get ahold of your heavy breathing like you did on the treadmill and come back to a soft even in and out, your arms holding you up, bent forward over the low bench. You straighten up your body and lean back against mine for a moment, then grab your towels, wet and heavy on the tile bench of the steam room, and whip around. When your hand grips the handle of the door you catch my glance for a minute and give me that cute sly boy half smile, and then you're gone.

I sit on the lower bench for a moment, feeling my breath again, my body spent and tired and ready to go home. I rinse off quickly in the shower. You're still in the stall two doors down when I enter, but you've left by the time I am done.

I do a quick fix to my hair in the mirrors over the sink and you're almost done putting your faux-hawk back up in place behind me, our towels wrapped back around our waists, slung over our shoulders, as if nothing happened, when a woman walks in with a start. "Am I...what are you...wrong...uh?"

We catch each other's eyes in the mirror. Usually this type of thing gives me butterflies and cause for concern. Usually I am an impostor in women's bathrooms and locker rooms; usually I am seen as an outsider, potential predator, problem, misfit, outlaw. But here there are two of us, and we just chuckle as she very obviously scans our bodies for signs of hips and breasts and then, embarrassed to be staring, scurries off.

By the time I'm done with my hair and emerge into the changing room where the lockers are, you're dressed and shoving your gym clothes into a barrel bag. You make a point of coming over to get a tissue right next to where I'm standing, unlocking my locker.

"I don't usually...uh..." you stammer, not talking to me but talking near me, keeping your chin low, shifting from foot to foot. Your handsome face gives you away: you're a pretty boy, and you date pretty girls. Not hunky butches.

"I know," I say. "Me either."

Your eyes twinkle as you look at me one last time. "See you around," you toss over your shoulder. "Good workout."

LUCKY NUMBER THREE

Beth Wylde

To Peggy, the world's most amazing fan. Remember the Doctor's orders. No more unsupervised hockey games!

Whoever coined the phrase, *third time's a charm*, should have his ass kicked. This is our third attempt to win the championship, and though we're making the other team really work for the title this year, the odds of us winning are not good.

We're all tense as we watch Brooke, our right wing, race down one side of the rink with the puck guarded tightly in front of her. We desperately need her to score. We're down by one point and time is running out.

Like a bat out of hell, one of the opposing players moves in beside her. A warning roar goes up from the crowd but it's too late. Number twelve's stick connects with Brooke's lower leg and she goes down in a heap. The referee blows a whistle on the penalty, sending number twelve to the box, but the damage has been done.

"God damn it."

Coach's profane exclamation isn't unexpected. We all just witnessed the incident firsthand and share her frustration. While number twelve is grinning as she makes her way to the penalty box, Brooke takes her time getting up. It's obvious that she's favoring her right ankle.

"Tanner, you're in. Cross is out. Get your ass out on that ice."

I hop up off the bench, clutching my stick from more than just anxiety. My knee is killing me. It throbs in time with my heartbeat and only my stick and my resolve keep me standing. I have plenty of experience dealing with pain though. We all do. Hockey is not a gentle sport.

Desire is my sole motivator now. This is it. My last chance to be on a championship team. I don't have time to be hurt. I've got a job to do, and nothing, not a damn thing, is going to keep me from it.

My body has been sending me gentle warning signals for months, but subtlety is not one of my strong points. I've ignored every ache and pain, pushing myself harder than ever before through each practice and game. I'm not going to be able to ignore the signs much longer. What I'm feeling now is anything but subtle.

"All right, Steph. One point. One frigging point. That's all we need."

Coach's gruff voice snaps me out of my funk and I turn to face her for last-minute instructions. Her deep tenor matches her build. Like most of us she's tall and thick and built to brawl. Tiny, tender women don't survive very long in our world.

At five foot seven I'm actually the smallest member on our

team, but I've still got enough power and muscle to back up what comes out of my mouth. I've yet to lose a fight. On the ice or off.

Coach's directions leave me confused, but I have to choose my words carefully. Aggressive attitudes are part and parcel of the game, but Lyza is famous for her sideline outbursts. She has a nasty temper and she doesn't like to be questioned.

I take a deep breath and let my inquiry fly. "We're down by one. Should I try for two goals instead?"

Coach shakes her head. She's too deep in the zone to be pissed. Thank god for small favors. "Not enough time left. We've got just over a minute. I'm not worried about winning right now. Go for the tie. We can beat their asses in overtime. I want that fucking trophy."

Her command leaves no room to argue. I nod in understanding and slam my helmet into place before heading out onto the ice. Brooke is on her way toward me, prepared to warm my empty spot on the bench. The look on her face is equal parts pissed and pain. I know exactly how she feels.

As we pass side by side she brushes against my shoulder. "Crush those bitches."

Her plea is a war cry in my ear that leaves my blood boiling. Brooke wants this win almost as much as I do. Losing is not an option. Not anymore. I'd do just about anything to win. I hope the devil isn't standing somewhere close by with an offer for my soul. At this point I might just sign it over.

As I skate into place the announcer breaks the situation down to the crowd. We have the home-ice advantage so he is rooting for us to win. It's a nice perk. "Tanner comes in for Cross. Penskey gets two minutes in the penalty box for that underhanded move she just pulled. Cross seems to be limping a bit. Let's hope she's okay."

The crowd erupts in the stands as the referee raises the puck high then drops it. Game on. As we fight for possession the fans go insane. The noise inside the arena is nearly deafening. Sweat stings my eyes and the adrenaline level is in overdrive. My leg gives a twinge to remind me of my stupidity, but I push past it. There will be plenty of time to recuperate once the game is over. If we win I might even give retirement a thought. Coach has been looking for an assistant and I know I can do the job. Younger women keep popping up every season and it's getting harder and harder to compete against them. I refuse to leave if we lose, though.

A quick glance at the scoreboard reveals we have forty seconds left. I've got control of the puck and my teammates plow me a path down the center of the ice. It's now or never.

I'm almost close enough to try for the goal when two members of the opposing team manage to break through our defense. They veer off to surround me, one on each side, and gaining fast. I know I'm in trouble. Just a couple more feet and I'm guaranteed to make the shot, but from where I am, it is still too risky. If I miss, the game is over. No time to try again.

Then Mulligan, our right defense, is rushing to my rescue. Dee Mulligan, number three, is the biggest, baddest, butchest player in the entire league. I thank god every morning that she's on our side. I wouldn't want to face off against her for all the money in China. That scenario would be all the retirement incentive I'd need, whether my knee was screwed up or not.

It doesn't hurt that Dee is also really nice eye candy. She's tall and muscular with dark skin that hints at something more than just white bread in her family tree. Her black curly hair is cut really short in the back and there's not an ounce of fat on her frame. Dee has starred in more than one masturbation fantasy of mine. It's impossible to watch her at play and not get turned on. She's a beast on the ice. Aggressive to the max. Team showers have been especially stressful. It's all I can handle to see her parading around the locker room half naked and totally unashamed. Her body is a work of art.

She turns to the side and flashes the big number three painted on her back as she aims one beefy shoulder at the woman barreling down on my right. I wince in sympathy as they make contact. Even over the roar of the crowd I can hear the impact. The girl goes down in a tangled heap of her own arms and legs, spinning madly until she hits the wall with a meaty thud. She's definitely going to feel that in the morning. Hell, she's probably feeling it right now.

The woman on my left is in collision range and there's no one to hold her off. I rear back and smack the puck with every ounce of strength I've got. Before I can follow its path the bitch hits me hard and we both go down. My knee sends up a final plea for mercy as it is wrenched to the side. Based on the lightning bolt of agony that shoots up my thigh I know I'm done for good.

My ears start ringing and I worry I'm going to pass out. Then I realize it's the crowd. The fans are going nuts. Dee reaches down and grabs me up off the ice like a rag doll, shaking and spinning me like I weigh absolutely nothing. To her I probably don't. God she's huge, and even bigger up close. All muscle and solid as a rock. She's jumping up and down, screaming like a banshee. Either I actually made the goal or she's gone crazy from the pressure to win. Both scenarios are a possibility at this point.

The announcer clears up my confusion. "Oh, my god! Tanner makes the goal with only two seconds left! It's a tie! Three to three!" He is shouting to be heard and even then it's tough to make out the words if you aren't listening closely. "We're going into sudden death overtime. I can't believe it folks. We just might win this one."

"Hot damn, Steph. You did it. You really did it! That was the coolest thing I ever saw. You really whacked the shit out of that puck. We're gonna win!"

Dee spins us around once more and then sets me back down on my skates. I grab her shoulders to keep from falling as a girlish squeak breaks loose from my lips. She frowns and immediately hoists me back up. "What's wrong? Are you okay? I didn't hurt you, did I?"

I shake my head, but I can't talk yet. It feels like hot lava is being poured into my kneecap. Putting weight on it has made it worse and I'm fighting hard not to barf on Dee or the ice. What a mess that would make. If I have to quit that's definitely not the thing I want people to remember about me.

"My knee. Aw, shit! I think I broke it when that bitch hit me."

The grunt I emit this time is a little more dignified, but not by much. Dee doesn't say a word, just slowly starts moving us toward our box. The team doc is standing by as coach helps to maneuver me off the ice and onto the bench.

The minute Dr. Grey touches my leg I let loose with an unholy shout and a string of expletives that would make a sailor blush with shame.

"Son of a fucking bitch. Shit. Damn it all to hell. Don't do that again!"

The doc ignores me and continues to poke and prod at my leg, going so far as to cut away my uniform until he reaches bare skin. The swelling is already noticeable and it's turning an ugly shade of purple. By tomorrow it will be black and blue.

Coach is hovering close by and her mother hen routine tells me more than the doctor's ugly frown ever could. I won't be getting back onto the ice anytime soon. If ever.

That realization, more than the pain, is enough to make me cry. The first few sobs manage to escape before I can get control of myself. Everyone nearby pretends not to notice, it's a jock thing, but Dee is pressed close to my side and I know she heard me.

The doc looks up, past me, to coach. "I need to get Tanner to the locker room so I can get a better look."

Lyza asks the question I'm too scared to put into words. "What's the damage?"

"Definitely dislocated. I don't detect a break. Could be some tearing or a hairline fracture but I can't tell for sure without an X-ray. If we can get her to the locker room the ambulance can take her to the hospital from there. I'll call ahead and let the emergency room know she's coming in. I have a friend on duty tonight."

Oh, hell no! I'm not leaving yet. I shake my head in protest. "Nope. Not happening. I'm staying right here."

The coach leans over my shoulder and gets right in my face. Her cheeks are pink with the first hint of anger. "You're going to the hospital and that's final."

Normally I'd just nod and do what Lyza tells me but not now. I'm already out of the game, so I'm not sure what else she can do to intimidate me. Whatever she has in mind is not going to work tonight. "Sorry, coach. Not right now." My temper is running close to the edge. Everyone's is. I try for some damage control. "I'm not trying to be a hard-ass, but I got hurt scoring the game tying point. I want to be here until it's over. I want to watch us win. Then I'll go wherever you want me to."

Doc chimes in before coach can get a word out. "You're not staying in the box. That leg needs to be elevated to help slow the swelling. The joint needs to be realigned and pushed back into place as soon as possible. That can't be done here."

He has a point and I know it. I just don't like it. I have another idea. "We've got a few minutes before the final round starts. Cart me back to the locker room, do what you have to do, then get me back out here to watch us beat those bitches. Afterward, I'll take the ride to the hospital. How about that?"

Doc shakes his head. "You have no idea how painful a procedure like that is. I don't have the type of drugs on hand to keep you comfortable. Go to the hospital and we'll call you when the game is over."

I'm getting pissed now. "I didn't ask you to make it painless. I asked you to fix me enough so I can stick around to watch us win. When coach has that fucking trophy in her hands I'll go to the emergency room and not a second sooner. Are we clear?"

Doc intercepts and grabs coach by the arm, pulling her to the far end of the box where I can't hear what's being said. Her face is so red, I'm worried her head might explode. As one the team glances over at coach. They know when to beat a hasty retreat. They scramble off the bench and dash to the locker room. Strangely Dee doesn't go with them.

She's almost as close to me as she can get without sitting in my lap. Somehow, though, she manages to get closer, leaning her head next to mine until I can feel her warm breath against my neck. Her lips brush the shell of my ear and I shiver from head to toe.

"Are you cold?"

"N-n-no." I hope she attributes my stutter to my injury even if it isn't because of that.

"Are you in a lot of pain?"

Hmm? That seems like a rhetorical question but I answer anyway. "I've been better. It's actually starting to go a bit numb. I don't know if that's a good sign or not, but it beats the way it felt while you were dragging me off the ice. Thanks for that by the way."

It feels stupid to say thank you without looking Dee in the

face but I know if I turn my head our mouths will be dangerously close to touching. I don't trust myself not to close the
distance and press my lips to hers. I've dreamed of doing it all
season. I know she'll kiss just like she plays. Hard. Full out. No
holds barred. I'll bet she fucks the same way too. I shiver again
just thinking about it.

"You're welcome." She tentatively puts one large hand on
my thigh. When I don't protest she keeps it there, moving a bit
higher until she hits the junction where my leg meets my groin.
I start to shake slightly and can't seem to stop. "I thought you
weren't cold."

I groan. "I'm not." I'm so fucking turned on I could almost
come in my pants. The throbbing in my clit is a welcome
distraction.

Doc and Coach pick that moment to return. I don't know
whether to be grateful or pissed. One more minute and I might
have embarrassed myself by begging. Dee's hand stays on my
thigh. If they notice they don't say a thing about it. Coach looks
calmer as she kneels down until we are eye to eye. I don't know
what Dr. Grey said to her but I'm eternally grateful.

"Dr. Grey and I discussed the problem. First off, you are a
stubborn little shit."

I nod. That's no newsflash to me. My mom would agree too.

"I understand why you want to stay, but I don't like it. It's
your body though, so the choice is yours. You can do what's
best and let the paramedics take you to the emergency room or
Dr. Grey can treat you in the locker room and you can wait out
the last period there."

"The locker room? No! I..."

So much for calm. Coach gets right up in my face, her cheeks
going from light pink to scarlet in a nanosecond. The barely
controlled fury is evident in her voice. "It's the locker room or

the emergency room. Take your fucking pick!"

Dee's hand on my leg tightens and I know I'm out of options. The choice is simple. I look over at the doc. "You ever done this before?"

He nods. "Twice. Once in the hospital and once at a game. The one at the game didn't turn out so well."

I shrug. "Third time's a charm. Let's do this."

Dee wraps an arm around my shoulders and all but carries me back to the locker room. Whatever meeting the team is having breaks up as we enter. As they make their way back to the arena, they each acknowledge my sacrifice in their own special way. A pat on the back. A smile. A promise of victory. That's the one that thrills me the most.

As doc positions me on a nearby therapy table Dee seems jumpy. When he walks off to gather supplies Dee moves in close once more, sliding between my spread legs. The thought of her doing it naked, with a thick cock strapped on and ready to fuck me, leaves me no choice. I reach out and snag her by the back of her neck. The move takes her by surprise; which is probably the only reason I'm able to budge her. When she realizes my intent she doesn't resist. The resulting lip-lock is brutal. Both of us fighting for dominance. It's the jock mentality. We don't like to submit.

I let her know with my teeth and tongue that I'm in control right now. If we manage to get naked and horizontal I know who will be on the bottom and I'm okay with that. I just want to make her work for the privilege of being on top.

Forget medical attention. My knee doesn't hurt a bit anymore. I feel like I could take on the whole opposing team by myself. My nipples spring to attention and only the thick uniform hides my excitement. My clit is pulsing and one touch is guaranteed to send me over the edge. I'm wondering how to get Dee's hand into my pants when Dr. Grey sneaks up. I don't hear him until it is too late.

One second I'm in heaven and the next I'm in hell. A quick snatch and grab on my leg is all the warning I get before Dr. Grey pushes my kneecap back into place. I pull my mouth away from Dee and scream.

Dee latches back on to my lips and swallows my protest. When we finally come up for air doc is grinning. He shrugs unapologetically. "I knew it would go back into place easier if you weren't tense. You seemed pretty relaxed when I walked back in, so I went for it." He pats my leg and my immediate reaction is to kick him in the nuts. I refrain somehow and realize that my knee really does feel a lot better. It still hurts but nothing like when I first fell.

"Do I still have to go to the ER after the game?"

"I highly recommend it. I have to get back out to the ice in case someone else gets hurt. I expect this last period to be rather rough."

As Dr. Grey makes his exit I feel nervous about being all alone with Dee. What if she and Dr. Grey planned this whole scenario? I don't think I can handle knowing that she led me on just so the doc could fix my leg easier.

The concern in my expression must be clearly visible. Dee snatches my face in her hands and kisses the doubt right out of me. Unless she is vying for an Oscar there is no way she's faking the desire I feel burning between us. Now that my knee is relatively stable, sex is the only thing on my mind. I want to come so bad I can hardly stand it. I want to bury my face between Dee's legs and suck her clit until she creams all over my face then beg her to do the same. There are a hundred different kinky scenarios running through my mind, but I know our time is limited. Judging by the noise of the crowd the game has started back up. The first team to score a goal in overtime wins. I love my teammates but I don't want them to walk in on Dee and me having sex. I'm also too greedy to wait.

I pull back and start kissing my way down her chin, nipping at every available inch of skin I can find. She's grinding her hips against me while one hand works its way under my jersey. One deft flick of her wrist and my bra is undone, my breasts loose beneath my uniform. Dee doesn't waste any time. She pinches my right nipple, pulling and twisting until I can't take it anymore.

"Please!"

She nibbles on my earlobe. "Please what?"

"Touch me. Make me come. I'm dying."

Her voice sounds pleased. "All you had to do was ask."

Her attitude is cocky and I know I should be pissed but I'm too horny to care. If she doesn't touch me soon I'm going to reach down and do it myself. I start to do just that.

She smacks my hand away, and then her fingers are suddenly where I need them most. I'm so wet she actually slips past my clit. As she moves back into place I reach for her waistband. She stops me with a stern look and a tug on my clit.

"You can do me later. Right now I want to watch you squirm. I can't focus if I'm busy riding your fingers, and the first time you make me come I want it to be in your mouth."

"Oh, shit, yes!" That's it. I'm done. Her explicit talk and steady manipulation of my clit has me crying out my orgasm for the world to hear. I wrap my arms around her waist to steady myself as I shudder through the final waves of my climax.

"Jesus Christ." She pulls her hand free and starts licking her fingers. We both jump as the announcer and the crowd start screaming. He must really be hollering for us to hear him so clearly in the locker room. "They've done it. Oh, my god.

They've won! The Bears are the new district champs!"

Soon the locker room is full to bursting. The atmosphere fairly glows with excitement. Doc is still insisting I go to the emergency room, but I don't mind so much anymore. We won, and Dee plans to follow behind the ambulance so she can take me home afterward. There's no doubt about it. Three is definitely my new lucky number.

GIVE AND GO

Anna Watson

E lsie and I had gotten good at quickies. We had to be, with our
six-month-old twin boys in command of 99.9 percent of our
home time. Today, Nate and Terry were miraculously napping at
the same time, and the moment had finally come. My wife, fresh
from a shower, was folding baby clothes on our bed. I threw
her down onto the pile of Onesies and yanked open her bath-
robe. Her plump breasts spilled out invitingly, but I paused only
briefly to enjoy the sight. Already turned on and breathing hard,
Elsie spread her legs, reached down to pull aside the crotch of her
panties, and I was in. For foreplay, we'd had weeks of teething, an
endless cycle of passing each other in the night as we walked and
rocked our miserable sons, smiling helplessly at each other when
we met in the kitchen where we were forever rummaging in the
freezer for a frozen teething aid. I was so horny *my* teeth hurt. I
drove into her with a desperate abandon other parents will recognize: we missed each other, we wanted each other, we needed it
bad; the baby monitor was on, and the clock was ticking.

It didn't take long before we were both completely in the zone. We had started out trying to be quiet but soon threw all caution to the winds. As I sucked on Elsie's earlobe, my hands busy with her nipples, she was working herself up to her own special, sexy, orgasmic yodel, and I was grunting and hooting like a damn gorilla. This was going to be a good one, one of those fucks when we both came at the same time, when our energy and the stars were aligned in some mysterious and glorious fashion, when the fucking and the coming were equally intense, when we were one with the elemental fuck energy, the universe blessing us with seamless connection: butch and femme, wife and wife, parents, lovers, friends, god and goddess; yes, here it was, here it was!

The phone rang.

I tried to ignore it, pumping even more frantically, but Elsie had already looked.

"Your sister," she said.

I slumped against her, burying my face in her bosom, wishing Caller ID had never been invented. I knew I would have to take it, though. It was probably about Dad.

Lately, Dad had been falling. He would be eighty this year, and Bev and I had been working to convince him to move to an apartment in an assisted-living complex. After this last fall down the back steps, he had finally agreed to go, which was why Bev was calling, and which was why, the weekend after that almost-transcendent quickie, I kissed my wife good-bye and drove down to Virginia to help him move. Bev, who lived one town over, was waiting for me in the living room of Dad's house, the house we'd grown up in.

"He's at bingo," she told me, after we'd hugged. "But he's started."

"No kidding!" Piles of books, papers and clothes were everywhere, the kitchen cupboards had been dumped and I could see out the window that every tool from the garden shed was tossed onto the lawn.

Bev grimaced. "He's already put the house on the market," she said. "I think he wants to get rid of everything."

In order to process this information, it seemed best to go out for coffee immediately. It was lucky we did, because we found a flyer at the Java Jump calling for donations to an upcoming yard sale, benefitting the Lady Redwings, the women's soccer team at Mary Jackson.

Mary Jackson used to be a women's college here in town, but had recently opened its doors to men. This infuriated me; what, sexism has disappeared from our world? It's obvious we still need women's colleges, but no one had asked me. At any rate, MJ had played a large part in Bev's and my early lives: it was where Dad taught math for forty years and where we had gone for undergrad. These days, however, I hardly ever spared it a thought.

"This is great!" Bev said, pulling down the flyer and tucking it into her purse. "After Dad gets done simplifying his life, the team will be all set. No one else will have to donate a thing!"

"Lady Redwings—what bullshit!" I said. "In my day, we were just the Redwings."

"I know, mine too." Bev hadn't played soccer, but she was in solidarity with me. I'd played varsity all four years.

It had been much less painful than I'd expected to empty out Dad's house, certainly less painful than helping him purge the place of Mom's things after she died. Then, he'd just sat in his lounger, his eyes open, staring at nothing. Now, he slipped off to hang with his cronies, cheerfully directing us to "get rid of all this crap!" We rented a U-Haul, and by Monday the house was empty and the trailer was full. I called the Lady Redwings

Booster Club to let them know we were ready to come by. Dad and Bev offered to stay and clean if I would drive the U-Haul over to campus to the drop-off site, and, foolishly, I agreed.

I had visited Dad hundreds of times since graduating from Mary Jackson in 1987, but I had never, ever, felt the urge to visit my old school. Despite how much I'd loved playing for the Redwings, by senior year I was desperate to get away from the repressed and repressive atmosphere of MJ, where being queer was an invitation for nothing but pain and misery. Why revisit the site of so many humiliations and so much heartache? I had no need to take a nostalgic tour of the stately student health building, for example, no matter how architecturally pleasing, as that was where a counselor once told me she was sure I would feel less depressed if I just gave men a chance and stopped making my classmates uncomfortable with my unfeminine style and behavior. I also didn't need to remember all the girls who were "gay after dark" or "gay when drunk" or "gay until grad-uation" or, the worst of all, "gay with you one time and one time only." I wanted to be gay all of the time, and that's why I moved to DC as soon as I could.

No, I didn't need to relive those salad days, and most of all, I didn't need to remember my deep and painful problem with straight girls. I'd had it really bad. All through high school and on into college, I fell in love with my straight soccer teammates, the flick of their ponytails, the twinkle in their eyes, their viva-cious breasts and breathy laughter. They, in turn, about killed me, flirting with me like crazy, teasing me into a frenzy. I never stopped hoping that if I just held out long enough; was nice enough, enough of a good sport, a good friend, I would finally get a real kiss, and they would finally let me make love to them. What I got instead was the assignment of designated driver, while they got wasted and gave their boyfriends blow jobs in the backseat. And wasn't it me, good ol' Selena, who was always there, holding their hands, when the boyfriends dumped them? Of course it was. If I wasn't desired, at least I could be useful. At a certain point in my life, I assumed that was all I would ever get. Who wants to be reminded of that shit?

So when I found myself driving around the side of Tauton Hall, where we used to sneak onto the fire escape and drink, I was feeling very tense. The Booster Club kids were friendly and full of energy, though, nice guys. They told me the Lady Redwings were about to practice, and after we were done unloading, I surprised myself by jogging over to the sports field.

The smell of the pitch, the freshly painted white lines—things hadn't changed much. I'd taken a break from my over-40 soccer league back in DC when the twins were born, and jogging around the perimeter of the soccer field made me realize how much I missed it. I fucking love soccer. Always have. I'd slowed down a bit, but in college I was on fire.

Back in my Redwing days, I was known for being a solid utility player, someone who could run all day with good pace, someone you could count on. Goal assists and creating plays were my fortes, along with laser-like concentration, a slightly insane disregard for my own personal safety, and an ability to assess the whole field quickly. And team loyalty. I loved my teammates. All those sexy straight girls.

As I lingered on the sidelines, the current Redwings ("Lady" be damned!) ran out onto the field, warmed up, and began to scrimmage, their strong bodies beautiful in the bright afternoon light. A freckled redhead with a long, curly ponytail, glanced my way, then made a beautiful chest trap, redirecting play so that her team scored a goal. It gave me goose bumps, and I shouted, "Yes!" The redhead looked my way again, and I could have sworn she winked.

* * *

Mary Jackson, 1984: I'm running around the track, cooling down after a tough game against the Yellow Jackets, our rivals. They defeated us the year before, but this year we won 2-1. I feel great, alive and horny, the way I always do after a game. Everyone is pumped, hashing over the goals, laughing, whooping. I'm trying to join in, but I can't concentrate because, as usual, Mindy Harper, right wing, number seven, is running behind me, keeping up a steady stream of nasty talk. I have no idea why she does this, but it's become a routine, one I both love and hate. Love because the girl is hot and I have a huge crush on her. Hate because she's drawing attention to me in a way that makes me want to die. Amber Mason, right wing, number eleven, is keeping pace with her, giggling and slapping her arm when she's particularly nasty. I have a huge crush on Amber, too. I run faster, pretending I can't hear them, but my butt feels ten times bigger than normal, an easy target for Mindy's extremely active imagination.

"Just look at that ass!" she says. "Big and juicy and jiggly. Mm-hmm, just look at those buttcheeks bounce. Damn, Selena, you have the most grabbable ass I ever did see!" She goes on like this for a few more yards until I put on a burst of speed, even though I'm supposed to be cooling down. I flop onto the grass next to Coach Cal, who's about to start us on our stretching routine, and Mindy shuts up. On the way off the field, though, she starts up again, and by the time we get to the locker room, she's picked up a few more teammates, all talking about my ass. As I scuttle over to my locker, I'm blushing so hard my eyes water, unable to escape the pack of giggling, snorting straight girls who crowd up behind me. I can feel the heat of their bodies as they brush against me, feel their breasts make brief contact with my back. I am utterly, painfully familiar with their breasts from having seen them naked more times than a baby dyke can be expected to come through and survive. Mindy has small ones, teacups, she calls them, and half the time she doesn't wear a bra, even in practice, which makes Coach Cal furious. Amber has double-D's, ripe and heavy, and even tamed by her sports bra, they spring from her chest invitingly. I try not to think about their breasts; try to smile, show them what a good friend I am, what a good teammate, how I can take their teasing good-naturedly. Oh, look, now they're taking turns trying to rattail me on the way to the shower. Love it. Hate it.

When I get back from the world's quickest shower, Amber calls me over. She's having trouble with her bra and wants me to tighten it for her, first while it's still on her body, and then, when my fingers aren't exactly steady, she whips it off and throws it at me.

"Come on, girl!" she orders, hands on hips, her liberated breasts lusciously swelling in the warm, funky air of the locker room. "Just tighten the left strap for me so I won't be all lopsided."

The reason she needs one strap tighter than the other is because her left breast is slightly smaller than her right. I'm always the recipient of this kind of private girl information, titillating and unbearable. In the locker room, my teammates talk openly and loudly about pubic hair, joking about patches and pelts, discussing which shape is most aesthetically pleasing to men (the upside down ice-cream cone is favored by most Redwings, although Amber herself enjoys a more natural look). They make detailed comparisons of tampons—crammers, Mindy calls them, just to see me blush, as I always do when the talk turns to girl parts. My teammates go on about leg shaving, pit shaving, crotch shaving. Share information about their boyfriends, if they're good in the sack or not, how stupid they are, what kinds of kissers they are, if they're romantic or not and what their dicks look like. I never knew dicks could curve before I was number two for the Mary Jackson Redwings.

Today is no exception, and the raunchiness quotient in the locker room just keeps mounting. Our victory talk is put on hold when Dora, the keeper, comes bounding out of the shower, screaming, "Look, I shaved my china! What do you think?" Everyone crowds around her, asking about razor bumps and what her boyfriend thinks. It's really starting to get rowdy.

I have a feeling of dread and anticipation in the pit of my stomach. It was an amazing game, and Mindy and Amber made some unbelievable plays together, including the first goal only three minutes in—a smoking through ball that cut the defense in half. They're our secret weapon. They look completely unassuming—Mindy, in particular, has a very nonchalant style—but they're a crazy machine on the field, working together like they have ESP. The skill of their give and go has to be seen to be believed. I love watching them, how Mindy's ponytail brushes her neck and shoulders as she casually surveys the available plays and then: Nutmeg! Shake and bake! Goal! And the killer look on Amber's face when she's taking the ball away from some lesser player is a true thing of beauty.

Everyone is going to have to blow off some steam after this game. We'll be meeting at Brenner's after dinner, of course, but there's usually a lot of what Coach Cal calls hijinks in the locker room first, and that's what I'm dreading. Anticipating. Really, it's sexual torture for me, but I don't yet have the words to explain it. All I know is that my stomach hurts and I'm so horny I'll come if I cross my legs or if one of my teammates playfully sits on my lap like they tend to do. Come hard and all over the place.

Packing up my bag in a fog of sexual anguish, I can't help

noticing that most of the team is still only partly dressed. Girls lean against lockers in their panties and bras, talking excitedly, some are still in the showers, and Mindy, wearing just see-through bikinis, is bent over, examining one of her teacups and expounding on her nipple and body hair theory.

"Blonde, brown-eyed girls like me usually have dark nipples," she says in a scholarly tone. I don't know if anyone else is paying attention to her lecture, but her words penetrate my brain like shrapnel. I can't stop listening, can't take my eyes off her lean, supple body. "Blonde, brown-eyed girls like me have very pretty dark nipples," she says again, emphatically, "but the thing is that there is a tendency to have a few hairs, long and silky and blonde, growing around those pretty nipples. You just have to stay on top of that and pluck them out." She lets go of the first teacup and begins to examine the other. "I'm doing okay right now, very smooth. So anyway, *brunette* girls with hazel eyes, like you, Selena, tend to have very pink nipples with no hair at all around them. What *brunette* girls have to watch out for is that they often have a little tuft between their boobies, which also has to be monitored and plucked out."

Sitting on a bench near Mindy, Amber is also just wearing panties, a tiny scrap of red cotton with a bow on the waistband. She's testing the bra strap I've finally managed to tighten and return to her. She looks up.

"You're so full of shit, Mindy!"

"No, it's true! I've been studying this very carefully!" Mindy raises her voice. "You guys! Come over here and tell me if I'm right or not!" Girls begin drifting over and Mindy trots out her theory again.

"Let's test it!" says Julie, who's usually pretty quiet, but who made the winning goal and is full of excited energy. She drops her towel, exposing her entire naked body, ice-cream cone,

medium-sized breasts, pink nipples and all. The next thing I
know, the entire team is standing around topless or completely
naked, looking at each other's tits. Even Andrea and Kelly are
in on it ("gay when drunk" and "gay after midnight just when
you least expect it" respectively). I'm backed up against the
lockers hoping no one will notice that I alone am fully dressed,
in my jean shorts, a sports bra, a muscle undershirt and my
Debbie Harry T-shirt. Everyone's so interested in each other's
tits that at first I think I'll be able to get away with it, even
get away completely, which is what I'm dying to do, almost as
much as I'm dying to stay. Amber, who once told me she used
to practice stripper moves when she was a little girl because
she thought it would be a glamorous occupation, is showing
Julie and Kelly how to shimmy. The three of them throw their
shoulders back and shake. And shake. The bouncing, juddering
extravaganza of titties, the impudent parade of panties and
pussies: I'm rooted in place. Suddenly Mindy is in front of me,
hands on my shoulders, her teacups pressed against my own
firmly bound-down chest.

"Ladies!" she shouts. "May I have your attention please?
One of our team members is not in compliance with the bosom
test!"

Immediately, I'm surrounded by the group of naked and
near-naked girls. They grab on to me, scold me, pluck at my
clothing.

"Take it off!" Andrea yells, and no matter how I fight,
I can't get away from them, can't stop them from pulling off
my T-shirt, rolling me out of my undershirt and finally, morti-
fyingly, unhooking me from my sports bra and exposing my
modest rack.

"Selena is a brunette with hazel eyes, and therefore..."
Mindy assumes a Carol Merrill pose in front of me while the

other girls hold me in place, keeping my clothes out of my reach, not allowing me to cross my arms in front of me.

"Pink!" they holler, as Mindy nods in satisfaction.

"Any tuft?" she inquires, and several girls get close enough for me to feel their breath, warm on my skin, as they examine my chest.

"No tuft!" Kelly reports, running her calloused fingers between my tits. "She must have plucked!"

"Did you pluck, Selena?" asks Mindy, motioning the girls who hold me to seat me on the bench. She leans over to see for herself.

"Fuck you." My voice comes out small and squeaky and I clear my throat. The girls force me down on the bench and Amber gives a little shriek and plops down on my lap, wiggling her ass and pressing her double-D's against me. I'm going to come, I know it. I make a heroic effort and manage to wrest myself away from my captors and jump up. Amber screams as she falls and I put out my arms to keep her from slamming into the cement floor, and then we all go down. I'm pushed and jostled, Amber falls on top of me, Mindy gives a rebel yell and flings herself onto the pile. Everyone is laughing and screaming. I can feel lips and noses, tits and hands, bellies and thighs and pussies touching my skin. Someone's finger is in my belly button, someone else's face is pressed against my neck, and I don't think it's my imagination that someone has my hand and is running her tongue over my palm and between my fingers. The cement is cold on my back, the scent of girls fills my nose— perfume, baby powder, shampoo, deodorant, lip-gloss, musk— and Amber is still pressed against me, stretched all the way out on top of me, straddling my leg, her strong thigh snugged up against my crotch. Masked by the commotion made by the pile of our teammates, she grinds down, pushing her cunt into my thigh. I buck up to meet her, my hands automatically cradling her ass. That's all it takes. I'm coming. Hard. All over the place.

Trembling, I push Amber away and thrash my way out from under the pile, managing to get up and stumble off a few paces. I crash into a locker and stand there panting, explosions still going off in my pants, my breath coming hard. My face, I know, is red and sweaty and guilty.

"Hey!" Mindy detaches herself and staggers to her feet, pointing at me. "She's getting away!"

Amber flashes me a look, curious, calculating. I see no love in her eyes. I turn and run.

We got Dad moved into his new place and promised to visit often. He kept saying he would be fine.

"You think he's really going to be okay in there?" Bev asked me as we hugged good-bye.

"Yeah, of course. He's a tough old guy." I sounded confident, but how could I know? Dad had already lost so much when Mom died, and now here went his home and privacy, his daughters off living their own lives.

On the highway heading home, I cranked an old Blondie CD. Mary Jackson was forever sending me information, eager to enfold me in their "family of fabulous alums," eager, also, for me to open my wallet. I wasn't interested, and I certainly wasn't going to give them any of me and Elsie's money. I didn't want to friend any of my old classmates on Facebook, either, although the idea of looking up Mindy and Amber crossed my mind every now and again. Really, though, I didn't want to see them smiling out at me, flanked by their husbands and children and dogs.

I let Deborah Harry's voice soothe me, thinking about my own family. I imagined how Elsie's face would light up when she saw me, how she would hand me whichever twin she happened to be holding, then grab up the other one so we could lean into each other for a family hug. After five years of marriage, it was something that happened automatically when I was sad or lonely or troubled—I would think about my wife.

I would think about her solid, curvy body, the way she looked after a bath, all rosy and relaxed, her hair wisping around her face, her expression dreamy. "Bubble baths are a strict necessity," she always told me. "That is written in hot-pink calligraphy in the *Femme Manual*."

Elsie's beautiful face, the sexy mole above her lip, the beginning of crow's feet around her lovely eyes, her laugh lines, her gorgeous auburn hair, her adorable, slightly sticky-outy ears. I could picture her so easily and so well, picture how she would welcome me when I got home, smiling, holding me in her gaze, her heart, her world of love.

PLAYING THE FIELD

Delilah Devlin

S weat stung my eyes. I lifted the edge of my blue jersey and
wiped my face, never losing sight of the black-and-white ball
flying across the short, crisp grass.

"One minute left!" Coach shouted from the sidelines.

It's just a damn game, I reminded myself, but still my
stomach plummeted. We needed one point to enter the penalty
phase—just one lousy point to tie this game up.

The Sharks were playing like damn minnows, letting the
Vipers kick our asses up and down the soccer field, our home
field. And from their grim expressions, every one of my team
members felt the same urgency. This would be the last game of
the season if we didn't win.

For me, it was about more than just the game. The last game
was also my last chance to work up my courage to do what I'd
been fantasizing about since the team had first started training
in early spring.

A green jersey bumped past me, the Vipers' player turning

her head to give me a smirk before loping off on her coltish legs down the field, following the ball. Anger flared.

One lousy point. I stretched my *shorter* legs, heart pumping so hard inside my chest the shouts from the sparse crowd in the bleachers faded away. My focus narrowed to the ball zigzagging from one Viper player to the next, my own blue-jerseyed teammates revealing the strain in their grim expressions as their movements lost fluidity and grace, and they clumsily tried to muscle close enough to steal away the ball.

I stretched one last time, edged up to the player dribbling the ball between her clever feet, swept out my foot—catching her ankle and sending her sprawling—then stole the ball.

I wasn't the most graceful player, wasn't the star, but I had the goddamn ball now. I lowered my shoulder and bumped a Viper out of they way, then pivoted on my toes and aimed myself and the ball toward the opposite end of the field.

From the corner of my eye, I saw her, backing up toward the other team's goalie box.

Vicky Moldina gave me a little wave, and I tipped my chin but didn't want anyone catching my intent, so I ran to the right, skirting their players, lowering my shoulders and putting on the bulldog face I'd been told intimidated the hell out of other teams—something that always set my own team to laughing, because they knew me better.

However, if they'd read the deadly intent in my heart, the searing determination, they'd have wondered who the hell I was.

My thoughts and heart slowed. I repelled the next player who moved in to steal the ball with a sharp, sly elbow. I charged forward, then zagged to the left, leaving two opponents to tumble over each other, and headed on a parallel path with their goalie.

Vicky backed up again, then shot toward the goal.

I kept on my parallel path, then tried a move I'd failed more often than I'd completed, kicking the ball with my heel to send it like a bullet to Vicky who was poised in front of the goalie's box.

Our star striker grinned, swept out her foot to catch it—but something happened.

Usually so graceful, her foot rolled over the top of the ball and her ankle turned. She fell in a heap to her knees, then beat her palms against the grass as a green-shirted bitch gave a whoop and stole the ball away, racing toward the other end of the field.

Three short whistles blew. I bent at the waist, hands braced on my knees as I dragged in deep breaths. My gaze remained on Vicky who pushed herself up from the ground. She met my gaze and mouthed, "Fuck."

I shrugged and forced a smile. "Just a game."

We shared small smiles while our teammates pulled together, remembered their manners, and gave Vicky halfhearted pats to console her before lining up to run past the other team, slapping hands and offering insincere congratulations.

I ran behind Vicky, wishing I hadn't passed the ball to her. Not because I was disappointed with the outcome, but because I didn't want this to be the memory she took away from the game. I didn't want our friendship tainted even a little bit.

After we huddled with the coach and offered each other hugs, I trudged toward the showers in the rec center.

"Dinner at Hooters!" Coach called out, and I grinned. We'd have had Outback if we'd won; Hooters had been meant to spur us toward victory.

As players headed to their lockers, Vicky limped toward the coach's wire equipment cage. She dug beneath balls and netting, then pulled out the first aid bag.

"Did you hurt yourself when you took that tumble?" I asked, my voice a little thick because hell, it was *her* I was talking to.

"It's my knee. I felt something pull."

"Do you need to go to the emergency room?"

She shook her head, sweaty tendrils of chin-length black hair shaking against her cheeks. "It's probably just a sprain. I'll wrap it after I shower." She pulled a rolled ACE bandage from the pack and started to put the bag back into the cage.

I reached for the bag, taking it from her, then grabbed a small jar of Tiger Balm and held it up. "I'll massage it before you wrap. It'll feel better faster."

Her brows furrowed—just a subtle motion, almost indiscernible, but the glance that swept my body was less so. Subtle, that is. "All right. After we shower."

After *we* shower. I know my jaw sagged just a bit at the way she'd emphasized that one little word. Drool pooled in my mouth. I followed her as she turned away, heading to her locker to pull out a plastic bag with her toiletries and a fluffy white towel. I did the same, hurriedly, a little nervous now.

I was reading too much into her words. Still, when we entered the open shower room, I hesitated before setting my items on the slatted wooden bench beside hers. When she raked her jersey over her head, I followed suit and stripped.

Most of the girls had already finished up. One by one, spigots turned off, towels slid around nude bodies, and they trailed out the door, leaving us alone.

Good locker room etiquette would have been to choose a spigot on the opposite side of the room, but when she strode to the far corner, out of sight of the open doorway, I followed, choosing one right beside her.

A small half smile kicked up one corner of her mouth before she turned her head, closed her eyes and let the hot water sluice over her hair and face, giving me the perfect opportunity to ogle her long, lithe body.

She squeezed shampoo into her palm, then handed me the bottle. With our gazes locked, we began to soap our hair.

Nothing had ever been this hot.

We'd both no doubt showered in open stalls in high school—naked women with slippery bodies—but I, for one, had never been this aware. With her hands raised, massaging her scalp, soap slithered down in long, winding ropes that caressed her shoulders, her small round breasts and taut belly. Her legs parted, widening her stance a little so that I could admire the small, smooth labia framed so perfectly by her muscular thighs.

"My knee's throbbing," she whispered.

My gaze darted up, and soap slid into my eyes. I grimaced and turned my red face into the spray before blinking back at her. Her lips were pursed in a smile; her eyes wrinkled at the corners with silent laughter.

God, if she was teasing me because she knew I was queer I thought I might never get over the embarrassment. But she turned, showing me her ass, and then glanced over a shoulder, one dark, arched brow raised. "It's okay for you to wash it. The others are gone."

"You sprain your hand, too?" I blurted.

Although my voice was gruff, she didn't seem put off. She squeezed soap from her short hair to trail down her back, then faced the white tiles.

I glanced toward the open doorway, but our teammates' voices faded away as they left. We were alone now. Free to do whatever pleased us.

I swallowed to hydrate my dry mouth, then turned back. Suds snaked toward her buttocks, and before they could disappear, I cupped them against her skin. Then I trailed my hands lower, enjoying the feel of her soft, tanned skin, which cloaked a muscular, rounded butt. My fingers dipped lower, raised each globe so my fingers could trace the creases at the tops of her thighs. Then emboldened by her soft murmurs, I slid a finger up her crack, pausing to play with the tight rosette before drawing away to dispense more soap into my palm.

Sliding up against her back, I reached around her, soaping her small breasts, my slippery fingers plucking her tight nipples. My touch grew firmer, more assertive, and I glided my palms down her belly.

Just when my fingers touched her mound, she turned her head. "Are you going to the dinner?"

"I'm not sure," I said, letting her know I was available for whatever she had in mind.

"Good. I could really use those hands of yours. My knee."

I withdrew my hands and stood back, a little confused. She'd allowed so much, invited it, but was she teasing?

I finished washing up as she walked away. She picked up her towel and watched me as I efficiently finished my shower then joined her. We both toweled off, then I followed her lead, wrapping myself in my towel and trailing behind her as we reentered the locker room.

She chose a padded bench and sat.

I picked up the Tiger Balm, grabbed another towel and folded it for padding, then knelt on the tiles in front of her. I lifted her leg and placed her foot in my lap, then unscrewed the balm and dug two fingers into the ointment. My thoughts calmed as I began to work it gently into the muscles around her knee, swirling it in circles.

"Have you ever touched your clit with that?"

Shock halted my fingers. "The Tiger Balm?" I snorted. "It burns."

"Be sure to wipe it off."

I swallowed hard again and kept my head down, because my

cheeks had caught fire. I deepened my massage, digging in my fingertips and the heels of my palm to ease the knotted muscles.

"Sometime, you'll have to give me a full body massage. You've got great hands."

"I'd like that," I said, careful not to let my rising excitement show too much.

When I'd finished, I leaned away to reach for the bandage, but halted when Vicky opened her towel and let it drape toward the floor. Her whole body was exposed, her legs parted, her pussy was warmly scented, smelling of soap, and *right there*.

"Your hands..."

I wiped them carefully on my towel, and then glanced up. "Is this just an after-game fuck?"

"Do you want it to be more?"

I nodded, holding her gaze.

"I liked the way you looked when you plowed through their defenses. Your expression was sooo...intense. I think that's what put me off my game."

"Sorry," I mumbled.

"It turned me on."

"Oh."

"I wondered if you'd be the same, that strong when you got a girl alone."

Straightening my back, I met her dark gaze. "I can be. I like it a little rough."

"So do I."

I canted my head, confidence at last soaring. This was going to happen, and she was giving me permission to take charge. "I'm gonna lock the door. Why don't you lie down on the bench? Make sure your ass is at the edge."

I stood, dropped my towel then strode to the locker room door. I peeked outside, but everything was quiet. I locked the door, knowing the coach had the only key, and that she'd already left for the after-game dinner.

When I returned, Vicky was lying on the bench, her hands resting on the floor. Her slender body was stretched, her back arched a little off the bench, her legs spread and her ass right at the end of the bench.

"Just like I like it." I came down in front of her atop my towel. Leaning toward her smooth cunt, I licked the length of her lips, enjoying the silky, pliant skin that was already reddening and growing engorged.

She tasted fresh, like seawater with a slight feminine tang. I burrowed my tongue between her lips and caressed her thighs as I delved deep into her opening, my eyes watching how her belly tightened and her nipples spiked.

Her legs moved restlessly apart, and I eased her thighs over my shoulders, taking control. I parted her lips, and plunged in again, rubbing my face into her slick folds, letting her juices coat my skin while my tongue flicked and lashed at the thin edges of her inner lips and her hard, hooded clit.

I cupped her bottom, then slid my thumb into her crack, pressing on her asshole as I centered my mouth over her clit and drew on it, sucking gradually harder and harder. I pushed my thumb inside her ass, then pulled and pushed the fat pad in and out. Between my thumb teasing her ass and my mouth drawing on her clit, her whole body vibrated with her building arousal.

Her hands came up and cupped my wet hair. Her fingertips dug into my scalp.

I pulled free, leaning back to watch until her eyelids fluttered open. "There's something I've wanted to do with you."

"What?"

"I need you to bend over the bench."

"You gonna spank me?" she asked, her voice deepening.

"It's my thing."

"You're a nasty little dyke."

"And you're not?"

"I like sex. Guys, girls."

"I don't mind sharing."

"Or watching? That's *my* thing."

I grinned wide, suddenly happier than I'd felt in long time. Freer. "We'll negotiate."

"I like the sound of that."

"Bend over the bench." I helped her into place—straight-legged so her ass rose high, and she balanced with her hands on the cold tile at the other side. I walked around to her and bent down as she looked up. I kissed her, letting her taste herself on my mouth, stroking my tongue into hers. When I drew away, I pulled on her bottom lip and bit it. "I love your mouth. After— I'll let it eat me right up. That knee going to be all right?"

Her lush mouth twisted in a wry grin. "Thought it was my ass at risk."

I dug into my locker for a shin guard, stripped the fabric from the padded, curved side, and slapped the plastic against my palm.

Both of her brows shot up.

I shrugged. "So I'll buy a new pair. It'll be worth it."

I walked around the bench, smoothed a hand over her pretty butt then drew back and gave her bottom a swat with the unprotected guard. It was flimsier than I liked, but still raised a nice pink line. Her pussy contracted. I stroked her cloaked clit with my thumb and laid another stripe on her bare butt.

Her ass tilted higher; her legs inched wider apart. I kissed her pussy, then stood slightly to the side to lay more narrow welts across both buttocks and the backs of her thighs while she grunted and mewled, her legs tensing, quivering, her heels rising off the floor then lowering as she tried to guess where I'd strike her next.

When I swatted low, grazing both thighs and her slick labia, she cried out. "Jesus, Carly! Fuck!"

Again, I swatted her cunt, then tossed down the shin guard, narrowed my fingers and thrust all four into her pussy. She was tight, but soaking wet, when I entered her, pushing inside while her flesh tunnel clamped around me. I feathered her clit with my thumb, then pulled my hand free, only to plunge deeper.

Her bottom rose and fell with each shallow thrust. Her feet braced wider apart. With everything exposed, cunt to pretty asshole, I folded my thumb into my palm and burrowed into her, ignoring her gasps. I swatted her buttocks with my free hand, light taps really, but enough to confuse her into relaxing, and at last, my fist slid inside her tight hole.

Her whole body quivered, and she whimpered. I bent, turning awkwardly, but got beneath her and stuck out my tongue to lick her clit while I screwed my hand slowly in and out.

"Carly, fuck..."

I felt a hot gush of fluid, wishing my face had been there to experience it and wondering if it would have squirted. I latched my lips to the top of her labia and sucked hard.

Her strangled shout echoed against the tile. Her knees gave, pulling her from my mouth, and I slowly withdrew my slippery fist.

When she lay sprawled across the bench, her pussy gaping, her ass a pretty, mottled pink, I bent over her and tongued every stripe then kissed her pussy, before pushing off her rump and walking away.

I pulled the netting from the coach's cage, and folded it, bunching it into a bed. I dragged it toward the metal whirlpool bath and placed my closed gym bag beside the pallet I'd made.

Vicky sat slumped beside the bench, eying my preparation. "That for me?"

"It's for me. I don't want you to hurt your knees."

Her dark eyes turned to smoke.

Following my instructions, she lay down on the net pallet, her head raised on a makeshift pillow.

I stepped over her, my feet on either side of her head, then wrapping my hands around the cool metal pipes running into the bath, I squatted over her face. "Now, lick me."

A fingertip trailed my slit. "I like your bush. It's bristly like a man's moustache."

I'd left a narrow fringe along my lips and atop my mound. "Tug it. I like a little sting."

Her fingers gripped the short curls and pulled. My cunt clenched.

"Baby, do that again."

Another reflexive clench tightened me right up. A finger entered me, swirling in my juices, then withdrew. I heard a sucking sound, but since I felt nothing, I guessed she'd licked her own finger.

I gazed down, amused to see just the top half of her face between my splayed knees.

Her head tilted, her tongue stroked out and caught the edge of the fleshy hood protecting my clit. She teased it with a flat-tongued stroke, then wrinkled her nose. "I've never been very obedient."

"You do know I'll have to punish you."

"I'll look forward to you trying."

Her face was so cocky, so assured, but she didn't know what kind of equipment I kept in my apartment. She also didn't know what I had inside my gym bag.

"Get me juiced up with that dirty mouth of yours. When I'm

ready I'm gonna fuck you, Vicky. Better than you've ever been fucked before."

"That's a big brag. Sure you can?"

I flexed my ass and rose an inch, then dropped slowly back down until my pussy rested on her mouth.

Her eyes narrowed.

"Suck it. Now."

She did better than that. Fingers prodded my ass and sank inside, her mouth latched on to my labia and wagged, tugging the engorged folds side to side. Then she nibbled them, making me jump and groan.

When her tongue stroked my clit, I drew in a deep breath and rocked on her mouth.

Too soon, the strokes fired me up. I straightened away from her. "Get your pussy on the hump. I need it up high."

Her face was a pretty rose, her lips swollen and wet. Her eyes were half-lidded and warm. She moved around, crab-like, laying her head so that it was lower than her hips. She braced her feet against the tile to either side of me.

I patted her plump pussy, gently at first, then with sharper slaps. Her legs tensed, toes curling against the tile. When she was juiced up, I bent over her body, against her open crotch, and reached for my bag. I unzipped it, fished inside and pulled out a long two-headed dildo.

Her eyes widened. Her breaths grew choppy. Her hands cupped her breasts and tweaked her nipples as she watched me push one end into my mouth to wet it, then feed the thick cock into her pussy.

I stepped outside her thighs, my legs bowed, and curved the dildo until the other end slid between my folds. Then with my hands gripping the pipes behind me, I raised and lowered myself, each downward motion pushing the cock deeper inside us both.

Her feet left the tile and her thighs splayed wide behind me. Only the cock connected us. I pulsed down, then up, then down again. When I ground down, our pussies consumed every inch of the flexible, thick shaft. Her taut, muscular belly flexed, lifting her hips to meet my thrusts; her legs swung upward and down, dancing her pussy against mine, grinding my bristly hairs against her engorged clit.

"Play with your tits," I said.

She complied eagerly, plucking the tight beads, pulling them then releasing them to spring back. "I have clamps at home," I said, watching her eyes grow dreamy and unfocused.

"I like clothespins. I'll bring them."

"I have a little suction cup for your clit."

"Fuck, *oh, oh, oh.*" Her thighs worked faster and faster as she rubbed herself against me.

The cock was so deep, her motions so hot, that my walls engorged, crowding around the shaft. When the rippling convulsions began, I bounced against her pussy.

With fingers plucking one nipple painfully hard, she slid her other hand down my belly then gripped my swollen clit with her fingertips and squeezed, pinching it and pulling it, adding the extra edge of pain I needed to slam over the edge.

I hung on the pipes, my arms aching in the their sockets, suspended as her pussy worked its magic, rubbing against mine, until at last her hips jerked, and she came with a raspy shout.

I let go of the pipes and came down on top of her, the dildo curving inside us, pushing against our walls for release. I kissed her, smearing her lips with an imprecise smooch, then nosed under her jaw to nibble at her chin and neck.

With our chests pressed together, we both groaned. Her arms came around me. "You're some therapist. I can't feel my knee at all."

Lazily, I flexed my bottom to grind my hips against hers. "Think you're up for the second half?"

I'd never showered so fast. We kept to opposite sides of the room, our backs to each other, but talked as we washed.

"My house is just off Bandera."

"I live in the Springs."

"Then I'm closer," I said, smiling because I couldn't wait to get her home and strapped to my bed.

"Then it's decided," she said.

Water stopped. I turned the handle to stop mine as well.

"No roommate?" she asked.

"Not in a long while."

"Then no interruptions. Good."

I glanced over my shoulder and caught her staring at my ass.

"What? It's cute. I couldn't help but notice."

I scraped my wet towel over my body and flung it into my bag. I wrestled to get my yoga pants up my legs then pulled a tank over my head.

Hands slid around me from behind, cupping my breasts. Her thumbs flicked my tight nipples. "Don't be mad, but I faked that fall."

Mad? With her pinching my tits, I couldn't work up more than a groan. "Why?"

"Like I said, it turned me on watching you plow through their line. I wanted all that intensity right between my legs."

I turned inside her arms and wrapped her in an embrace, hands sliding south to cup her firm ass. I swatted her butt, then pulled free and reached for my gym bag, which I swung onto my shoulder, in a hurry now to get her home. "I won't tell. I like how things turned out."

NO, TELL ME HOW YOU REALLY FEEL

ily goyanes

I sit by my tree every day and watch them walk by. Tall and with an easy confidence I would never have, they look like they were created in a lab or something. Definitely not your average human beings.

Especially the captain. She was just under six feet tall, with long, wavy brown hair that she kept in a ponytail almost 24/7, but I had seen it loose once when she was trying to bring up attendance at the volleyball games. The plan, apparently, was to walk around campus "engaging" the student body. Retch. She had come over to my tree that day and I, pretending not to notice her seventy inches looming over me, just kept sketching in my black Moleskin.

"Excuse me? I hate to bother you..."

I looked up at her from under my charcoal-lidded eyes. "Then why are you?"

She turned red and stood there for what seemed like a full minute. "Um..." She started to say something then thought better of it and walked away, mumbling an apology.

That's right. Walk away, cretin. Don't you know that jocks don't talk to emo art-school girls?

After that incident, she kind of tried to avoid me, but I would see her checking me out when she thought I wasn't looking. But I was. I always watched her, especially at the games. I know what you're thinking, an emo art-school chick attending a college volleyball game? Don't be so closed-minded. Brace yourself—I also watch the Super Bowl and the NBA championships. Don't let my sullen attitude and heavy black eyeliner fool you—I have school spirit.

I sit high up in the bleachers waiting for the game to start, dressed in tight jeans, sneakers, and a hoodie emblazoned with the school's crest pulled up over my head, obscuring my face. Yes, I have school spirit, but no one has to know about it. So, once a week during volleyball season, I don my "average person" disguise so I can attend the games without ruining my reputation with the coffee-house crowd.

The announcer starts calling out the names over the loud-speaker. This is my favorite part. "Number Twenty-Three and captain of the Lady Blue Jays, Julianne Murphy!"

She trots out of the hallway and into the gym/auditorium and stands there looking around. The bleachers are half empty, which is an improvement from previous games. I guess her efforts to engage the student body are working. She looks happy and I want to slap her. Doesn't she realize that there is more to life than sports? More to life than just refining your, admittedly hot, body? What about cultivating your brain? I shake my head. Jocks don't have brains, I remind myself. She dominates the court, spikes the ball into the faces of our enemies and brings home the win. I go home and rub my clit raw thinking about how much she annoys me.

* * *

She's eating lunch alone today. What a fucking miracle. Besides being stupid, jocks travel in herds. Especially Captain Murphy. There is always a group of sycophants around her, hemming and hawing, practically tripping over themselves to get closer to the golden girl.

She's sitting on a huge rock about ten paces from my tree and eating a wrap or some other trendy, pseudo-healthy lunch. Just looking at her makes me want to vomit. She looks my way several times pretending she's looking at something in the distance. What, Cap'n? Looking at the gym/auditorium to see if it changes color? I told you. Jocks are dumb.

I start sketching her. At first my strokes are sharp and deep, but then I lose myself in the sketch. I hear only pencil on paper—the entire school has disappeared. It is just me, my Moleskin, my pencil and my tree. She starts to take shape beautifully, almost as beautiful as she is in real life. I start shading when I hear someone clear her throat. Uh-oh. Captain Murphy must want to die.

"Is that me? I mean, the drawing, is that, um, a drawing of me?"

"Yes," I answer her. I am mortified, but I recover. "We're doing a project in one of my art classes and we're supposed to draw still lifes."

She seems to relax a bit, probably relieved that I didn't stab her foot with my pencil. Then something dawns on her, "But aren't still lifes..."

"Yes," I say acidly. "Exactly."

She turns red again, and if I hadn't known any better, I would have sworn that tears welled up in her eyes.

* * *

After the still-life incident, I didn't see her around for a week.
The Cap'n and her cronies must have taken a detour to the
gym/auditorium every day, because I caught neither hide nor
hair of her. We won the game that weekend. Murphy was on
fire; she was a woman possessed. Not a single ball got past
her the entire game and when she went up to serve, I could see
the other team cringe collectively. Our enemies did not score a
single point. Go team.

The following week, the jocks were back to their regularly sched-
uled programming. There was a new development as well. A
new girl, one I had never seen on campus before, was being very
touchy-feely with my Murphy, touching her biceps, stroking her
hair, and making slut faces at her. Being the dumb jock she is,
Murphy was basking in the attention. Although I did notice her
looking over at my tree several times....

We won the next several games and we were up for the state
championship. By the luck of the draw, I also had an interview
for an internship at a museum in the same city that weekend.
And by luck of the draw, I mean that all my scheming to get that
interview, in that particular museum, on that particular weekend,
had worked. Sometimes we have to make our own luck.

We ran into each other in the library the Thursday before the
championship game. I hadn't seen that cheap slut around, but I
was still boiling at the way Murphy seemed to enjoy the whore's
attention. Murphy sat at one of the long library tables reading
books on Andy Warhol, Salvador Dali, and for some odd reason,
Nan Goldin—who was an amazing photographer, but not a
painter. I crept up behind her real slow and stood there inhaling

her scent. She smelled like laundry detergent and wildflowers.

"Are you enjoying your picture books?"

She looked up at me in surprise and then a frown quickly consumed her face. I had never seen the captain frown and I didn't like it.

"I'm sure you're way smarter than me, and obviously way cooler, I mean you must have completely wiped out the shelves at Hot Topic, but I'm not dumb you know. I'm here on an academic scholarship, not an athletic one."

Well, well, well. The golden girl had some sass. Hot Topic? God forbid, that's where the *Twilight* crowd shops. I shop at thrift stores and estate sales. But, that was a good dig. Nice one, Cap'n.

"I didn't realize that they gave academic scholarships for finger painting. I do apologize." And with that epic line I turned to make a graceful departure, but she grabbed my wrist. She must have felt the same electric current that I felt when our flesh connected, because she stopped right when she was about to say something.

She shook her head as if to clear it of whatever she was thinking. "You shouldn't be so mean."

She looked so sincere, and for the first time ever, I noticed that her eyes were a light brown flecked with green and amber tones. I almost wanted to give in and say, "I know, Cap'n. I know I shouldn't be so mean. I just want you so much that it hurts."

Instead, I laughed. "I'm sure a big girl like you can take it, Cap'n. I just loathe still lifes."

I pulled away and she let me.

I went home and cried until I couldn't cry anymore. Once I got that out of my system, I fucked myself silly with my purple vibrator, reliving the close-up shot of her eyes on my face and the feel of her large, strong hand wrapped around my tiny wrist.

It's the weekend of the big game and I pack my car up for the four-hour drive. Murphy and her hangers-on are going on the team bus, I'm sure, but I will see her at the hotel. Of course I booked a room at the same hotel the team is staying at; what am I, stupid? I wouldn't miss even the possibility of seeing Murphy poolside, her light golden skin and perfect body in a bikini, relaxing before the big game. I'm bringing special toys with me for this trip—I have a feeling that Murphy is going to annihilate the other team tomorrow night and I'll be so excited that my pocket rocket just won't do.

The game was even better than expected. Murphy was all over the court, extending her body, jumping, diving and knocking the shit out of that poor, poor ball. The other team didn't know what hit them. I'll tell you, motherfuckers! You got hit by Hurricane Murphy, bitches!

I feel so alive on my way back to the hotel that I want to pull my car over to the side of the road and scream out, "We're Number One! We're Number One!" I feel like stealing a goat, painting it in our school colors and dropping it off at the other school's campus! Whew... I need to get a hold of myself. See, this is why sports are bad for society. They create a visceral reaction in our systems that takes us back to Cro-Magnon times. This isn't me... I'd much rather drink espresso while listening to The Smiths "Girlfriend in a Coma" on repeat. But I feel so good! It wouldn't kill me to have a small celebration in my hotel room, would it? I pull into a gas station and buy myself a four-pack of wine coolers. Woo-hoo! We're Number One! We're Number One!

* * *

At the hotel I get wasted, at least as wasted as anyone can get on two wine coolers, then I pull out my special red dildo, the one that has an extension for my clit so I can fuck myself and play with my clit at the same time. I replay the game in my head. Murphy serves and everyone gets the fuck out of the way. Murphy dives for a ball and hits it up so that one of her lazy teammates can send it back over the net. Murphy spikes the ball into the face of one of the losers from the other team. Murphy, Murphy, Murphy... I fuck myself thinking about her strong hands and golden skin. I think about her amazing eyes with their flecks of green and red, I imagine them looking into mine as Murphy rides my cunt with a ten-inch strap-on, pushing and pulling, her long, lean frame covering mine completely as we make love. I mean, fuck, as we fuck. My pussy starts twitching rapidly, then contracting, and I hold the image in my head, of my barely over five-foot body buried under Murphy, looking up at her and into her eyes as we both come at the same—BANG, BANG, BANG!

"What the fuck?" The knock comes again, louder this time. Not even thinking, I stand up and go look through the peep-hole. Uh-oh. Captain Murphy wants to die.

I am so livid, so enraged, so HORNY, that I just open the door and stand there naked, staring at her. When she sees me, she just stares at me with her mouth open.

"Come in you dumb ox, this isn't a show." I pull her in and shut the door quickly. As soon as I turn around, I get smacked in the face with what seems like eighty-proof oxygen. The captain is sloshed, ladies and gentlemen.

"Why...uh...why are you?"

"Naked?" I ask the normally agile, but now weaving Murphy.

"Y-y-yeah." She looks at me and I can tell that whatever she had planned in her drunken stupor did not include me standing buck naked in front of her.

I sit her down on the edge of the bed and take her shoes and letter jacket off. Standing in front of her with my hands on her shoulders I lean in and whisper in her ear, "Because I was just fucking myself thinking about your performance on the court tonight."

Apparently, forming an intelligible response is out of the captain's hands at the moment and she lifts me by my waist and sits me on top of her. God, she's strong. I start rolling my hips slowly and undulating against her body, brushing my tits against her face, softly sliding my nipples across her lips. Murphy groans and her fingers dig deeper into the soft flesh of my ass. "Put it in my mouth...please..."

I oblige my champion and place one of my hard, pink nipples in her mouth while I keep gyrating against her. She's a little sloppy, but mostly in control of her physicality. She rubs her teeth against my erect nipple, making me moan, and causing my already soaking pussy to secrete even more hot liquid, sticky fluid that is soaking into the captain's gym shorts as I ride her muscular thighs.

"I—I—always—wanted..." She tries to communicate what we have both been feeling, but I stop her. "Shh, Captain. Let's not waste time with words. You're here. I'm here. You won the championship game tonight almost singlehandedly and you have a naked woman sitting on your lap, willing to do anything for you. Just enjoy it."

And she did.

RUN, JO, RUN

Cheyenne Blue

R un, Jo, run. Down London streets that are never silent, even in the hours just before dawn. Run, Jo, run, your thirteen-year-old feet pounding the pavement, the breath hot and rasping in your lungs, your skinny body bursting with the effort of your heart. Run, Jo, run, away from home where your parents are screaming at each other again, screams that end with breaking glass, and broken ribs, and the wail of the ambulance siren.

Jo can't help her mother, although she's tried and the scars on her own body attest to her failure. So now Jo runs instead of fights, dodging the partygoers, and the late-night drunks, the shift workers alighting from big red buses and the occasional policeman who assumes a fleet-footed teenager must be a pick-pocket and gives chase but never catches her and never will.

Run, Jo, run, though the shadows of your life, away from parents, teachers and social workers who are supposed to care for you yet never manage to be there. At sixteen run from home and never go back. At seventeen run from the lover who promised to care for you but defined care as power. Run from the world, and learn eventually that the only constant is you and your body, its strength and speed.

Also learn that there are some things that you can't outrun: the horror when you learn you're pregnant, the sorrow when the baby is lost. And you can't outrun the knowledge that life is passing you by, and you're not ready for that. You're not ready to be a thief, a con, a prostitute, even though you know they're possibilities and they wouldn't be the worst.

So Jo stops running, long enough to enroll at technical college, long enough to learn that she has an aptitude for computers, long enough to return home and find her mother is dead and her father has captured a new lover. Long enough to learn and embrace her own sexuality.

Never long enough to fall in love. Never long enough for that.

And although she's stopped running from things that scare her, Jo knows she will never stop her *real* running. Not until her knees give out, not until she's shaky and feeble and can barely stagger a fifteen-minute mile. Maybe not even then. Running is when she is truly free.

She joins a running club, hoping to meet a girl like her, a girl with whom she can run, but the preppy insistence on teamwork and the slavish devotion to the stopwatch isn't her thing. After yet another evening nursing a glass of soda while conversation about road races she will never run flows past her, Jo leaves and doesn't return.

Her running, she decides, like her life, will be solitary.

And solitary it is. Jo moves to Staffordshire and discovers fell running. In the long summer mornings when the light slants golden over the ground by 5:00 a.m., Jo jogs along the road and then up the footpath that takes her over the tor. The heather brushes her ankles, and she has to watch her footing on the uneven ground, so she doesn't run as fast, but the freedom, the aloneness and the exhilaration it brings is worth it.

Run, Jo, run, along rough footpaths and bridleways, splashing through mud and soggy autumn leaves, run through the mist on the tor and the snow that lies thick and wet on the ground. Smile as a pheasant whirrs abruptly from under your feet. Bound down grassy slopes and attack the uphills, learn to embrace your solitude, learn to live your life alone. Run through winter and into spring again. A full year passes, and you are content.

One day, when she reaches the top of the tor there's a girl there. A girl like her, in shorts and a brief, bright singlet, with mud-splattered legs and dirty running shoes. Jo slows and observes her for a moment as the girl stretches her hamstrings methodically, her heel resting on the ordnance survey marker. The girl nods, Jo nods back and moves on, swooping into the downhill part of the run, leaping rocks and clumps of heather, splashing through the stream at the bottom of the valley, the girl already forgotten.

The next day, as Jo reaches the tor the girl is approaching on the other path. Jo slows enough to watch her powering up the final slope and sprint for the survey marker. The girl touches it, then bends double, hands on her hips as she drags air into her lungs. As Jo takes off down the hill the girl is once again stretching.

Jo doesn't see her for a couple of days, but on the weekend she's curious enough to time her run to reach the tor at that same time. There's no one there. Jo stops and stretches, but the other girl doesn't show. Oddly disappointed, Jo moves on, and runs an extra couple of miles instead.

But on Sunday, when Jo reaches the tor, the other girl is there. She's not stretching; she's jogging loosely on the spot. Her breathing is easy; she's obviously been there for a while.

"Hi," she says.

"Hi," says Jo in return.

"You run well," says the girl. "Do you mind if I run along for a while?"

"Not at all," says Jo, and if her heart leaps wildly in her chest she puts it down to the sprint to the top of the tor.

"I'm Carys," the other girl says.

"Jo."

Side by side, they lope down the slope to the wooded valley. Soon the path is too narrow to allow them to run abreast, so Jo moves in front. She can hear Carys's breathing behind her, the easy breath of the long-distance runner, hear the soft thud of her feet on rocks and dirt. Curious, Jo increases her pace until she's running faster than usual, and although Carys's breathing increases, she's still there on Jo's tail.

The path opens out again and they run side by side through the birdsong-filled wood, splashing through the stream, passing the occasional rambler. Two miles, three, four and their pace is still gradually increasing, until when they burst from the woods out onto the heath, they're flying and this is now no companionable run: it's a race.

The heath ends at a road, and Jo knows without saying that it will be the finish line. Three hundred yards, two, then one. Jo digs deep, focuses on the road, and ignores the heaviness of her legs, the way there isn't enough air in her lungs and the floating light-headedness that threatens to swamp her. She's aware of Carys at her side, matching her pace, sometimes half a stride ahead, and doesn't let herself believe that Carys is only pacing her and that she will break away in the last few yards.

They reach the road together and if there's a winner, Jo doesn't know which of them it is.

She crashes to the grass as exhausted as if she's run a marathon. Carys lies next to her, her body at an angle to Jo's. After a minute or so, Carys stretches out a hand, finds Jo's and grasps it.

"Great run," she says, and her breathing is nearly back to normal.

"Yeah." Jo lies still, listening to the thundering of her heart and savoring the touch of Carys's hand in her own. She wonders what Carys's touch really means, and then Carys squeezes her fingers, a swift caress with the pad of her thumb, and Jo wonders no more.

A routine develops. They meet at the top of the tor and run a few miles together, ending with the sprint to the road. Sometimes Jo wins, mostly Carys does, and then, if it's dry, they lie on the turf together to recover and share snippets of their lives: where they live, where they work, what TV shows they watch.

One day Jo asks, with a studied casualness, "You have a girlfriend?"

Carys squeezes her fingers and replies, "No. Not yet."

Throughout the days of summer and into autumn they run together. Sometimes they go farther, and the sprint for the road is replaced by long miles at conversational pace. Jo realizes she's falling in love, and the thought scares her somewhat. She knows Carys is waiting for her to make the first move, but that's the problem. Jo has no problem hitting on most women, but Carys is different. Carys could be more than a lover—she could be for life, and when Jo thinks of that, she gets a static buzz of white noise in her head and her mind spins onto other channels. Twice now, Jo has opened her mouth to say, "Shall we have coffee? Or a drink?" and each time fear has grabbed her tongue and forced the words back down.

And then one day, long into autumn, when the days are

getting so short that it's difficult to see the ground underneath their feet, Carys says, "We need to talk about this."

"This?" says Jo, and the beat of fear swells, and then subsides.

"It's too dark to see properly. I'm going to go arse over tit soon and be flat on my back on the heather. Where do you run on winter mornings?"

"Roads with street lighting," says Jo.

Carys smiles. "Me too. How about I come to your house tomorrow, and you come to mine the day after?"

Jo goes home and as she takes her shower, as she cooks and eats dinner, she practices asking Carys in for coffee. For breakfast. On a date.

It's raining the next morning, and the doorbell rings early, while Jo is still ramming her unruly hair into a ponytail and finding socks that match.

Carys bounds through the door when Jo answers it. "Nice." She has yet to look at the décor of Jo's small house, her eyes are fixed on Jo and Jo finds she's transfixed by Carys' direct gaze.

Carys comes closer. "May I look around?"

Jo nods, and straps her running watch onto her wrist. As she bends to pull on a sock, she sees Carys's slender calves walking up the hall.

Jo follows Carys to the kitchen, where the coffeepot stands ready to be flicked on after the run. Jo has thought long, and intends a casual "Fancy a coffee?" as they return to the house.

Carys comes closer, near enough that Jo can see her eyes are golden. Tiger's eyes, she thinks, with little dark flecks.

"It's raining," says Carys in conversational tones. "Do you really want to go for a run?"

"It hasn't stopped us before—"

Carys kisses her, swallowing her feeble words, kissing her as if she means it, as if she desires Jo, as if she wants her more than her next breath, more than the promise of a good run.

Jo's lips are slack for long moments as she wonders how they've come to this, why she hadn't done this weeks ago. But then her brain kicks into overdrive and she realizes it doesn't matter how they got to this point, or who initiated it. What matters is that they're here and now they can move on.

Carys's arms encircle her, smooth, hot and bare. Jo feels Carys's breasts, constrained by the binding sports bra, pushing into her own. But mostly, she feels soft lips and hands, strong hands starting to roam around her body: up to her shoulders, down her back to grasp her buttocks and pull her even closer.

There's a thrum in Jo's head, one of expectation and excitement. She breaks the kiss and says, "We've never skipped a run before, but if we go out now we'll get soaked."

Carys's eyes are dark and deep, the pupils so large that the dark flecks in her irises are nearly invisible. "I couldn't be wetter than I am already," she says.

Jo's mind spins to the bedroom, trying to remember how she left it. A mess, no doubt, with clothes and sports gear strewn around the place. But the sheets were changed last night and she doubts somehow that Carys will care about the mess.

She entwines her hand in Carys's and tugs her down the hall toward the bedroom.

The curtains are open to let the morning light in, and somewhere outside a bird is singing its heart out. Jo knows how it feels. The bed is unmade, but Carys doesn't seem to care and bends to untie her Asics. She pulls off her trainer liners and stands there in strong bare feet.

Jo sits on the edge of the bed and urges Carys toward her. She runs a hand up Carys's thigh—lean, strong, with defined muscles. Jo's fingers toy with the hem of Carys's shorts for a moment, before reversing course to meander back down. She notes how the tiny hairs, bleached blonde by the sun, are soft, and she traces her way down to curve over a calf muscle. Carys is lightly built and her running style is fluid and effortless. Yet her legs are like steel.

Carys places her hands on Jo's shoulders, her fingers digging tightly into the muscle in anticipation.

Jo leans forwards and moves Carys's singlet top up, enough that she can see her flat belly. Bending, she places her lips on the soft, quivering skin: wet open-mouthed kisses, tasting her girl. She pushes the singlet up farther, revealing the bright sports bra that covers Carys's small breasts. It's raspberry colored and matches her shorts.

Carys winds her hands in Jo's hair, tugging on the elastic that holds her ponytail in place until it comes free. Jo's hair cascades down in wild curls, and Carys sighs and pushes her hands into the mess.

"I've wanted to do that forever," she says.

Jo's fingers creep higher, until she's brushing the underside of Carys's breasts, then higher still until she's cupping their slight weight.

"And I've wanted to do this forever," she says.

She stands, and Carys's fingers fall away from her hair. In a swift movement she pulls Carys's singlet over her head, and tugs at the sports bra. It's elasticized, with no fastenings, and resists attempts to remove it.

Carys smiles, crosses her arms and pulls it up and off in a graceful motion. She stands, her arms high above her head, the bra wound around her hands.

Jo sees her slender figure, the small uplifted breasts and the illusion of restraint in the raspberry bra wound around her hands. Her stomach tightens at the thought, and for a moment she can't breathe as an image of Carys in her bed, her wrists bound to the iron headboard, fills her head. Then Carys shakes the bra away and the image is gone, and instead, there's the real Carys, naked except for the running shorts.

Jo lunges, white heat in her head, and her fingers and lips trace a path along that lithe body, until there's a nipple blooming between her lips, and her fingers are delving down, under the shorts, into the mesh liner and there's crinkly hair and soft skin underneath her fingertips. Carys doesn't shave, and Jo is glad. She loves a natural woman, and besides, grow-back is a bitch when you run.

Jo's own running gear, skimpy as it is, suddenly feels like too much. With shaking fingers she drops her shorts and pulls the singlet over her head. Her own bra is sturdier, more supportive than Carys's, the better to bind her fuller breasts.

Carys is watching her and there's a hungry expression in her face. "I've imagined you," she says, "your sports bra binding your breasts flat to your chest underneath a white shirt and black tie."

"I'll do that the first time we go out to dinner," says Jo, and then there's no more talking, only mouths and lips, fingers and hands, freckled skin and lean muscles.

They sink to the bed entwined in each other's arms and now Carys takes the initiative, unhooking Jo's bra and palming her breasts, rolling her nipples around in her fingers.

Jo is a creature of light and flame. Every touch of Carys's fingers on her nipples burns a molten pathway to her clit. She wants to be touched, wants to feel lips and fingers on her pussy, wants the jerking release of orgasm.

Carys moves in a meandering pathway down Jo's body, until she's poised between her spread thighs. In a swift motion she's between them, her mouth on Jo's sex, lapping in catlike motions at her clit. Carys's fingers push into the wet heat of Jo's cunt, and

Jo closes her eyes the better to focus the sensation. She knows she won't last long—this intensity, this heat, it's too much—and she comes in a keening wail, her belly rigid, her thighs jerking with the force of the contractions.

When the heat haze clears from her vision, Carys is looking at her, a hopeful expression on her face. Jo considers the long black dildo in the drawer, but not for long. This first time she wants Carys to fly apart under her fingers, wants to feel her heat and wetness, wants to sink wrist deep into her cunt, wants to see her come with the same blind intensity that she did.

Carys reads this in her eyes and swings a leg over Jo's hips, straddling her. Jo looks down along her body, sees where their pubic hair meshes together: Carys so blonde and fine, Jo so dark and wiry. She pushes her hand between them, palm up so that she can curl her fingers into her lover's pussy. Carys is wet, drowned wet, sodden like the fell after a summer rainstorm, slick and sweet. Jo moves her fingers back and forth, sliding easily through the moisture. She finds Carys's clit, caresses it with her thumb, even as her fingers clench and curl, stretching wide Carys's cunt.

She looks up, into Carys's face. Her eyes are closed, nostrils flaring. Jo pushes her fingers farther in, feels the channel tighten. She redoubles her efforts, circling the nubbin with her thumb, and feels Carys's thighs tighten around her hips and then the quiver inside, the ripples and internal shivers of orgasm.

Jo pulls Carys down so that their bodies are aligned. She strokes her sweaty hair back from her face and lets herself sink down into the lethargy after love.

For a moment she's scared; panicked that she can't do this, that her family's litany of bad relationships will drag her down; scared that her own poor history and the escape routes she's taken will suck her in, and that she'll run, run away from Carys, from the best thing that's happened in her life so far. Then Carys sighs and her fingers caress Jo's hip.

It will be all right.

Run, Jo, run. Along the quiet streets and footpaths, over the heather paths to the tor, brilliant in the morning sun. Run, Jo, run, let your legs take you far and fast, let your thoughts fly free. Run, with Carys by your side, your strides matched, the joy of movement in your veins.

Run, Jo, run, let the miles fly by, your lover and partner by your side. There are some things you can't outrun, and you don't want to.

Jo takes Carys's hand as they reach the tor and kisses her in the morning sunlight.

BOOT CAMP

JT Langdon

I was always on the pudgy side. *A sturdy woman,* my Turkish grandmother would say. *Curvy in all the right places* was how I liked to put it. Fat? I didn't use that word. It always seemed like an ugly word to me and I didn't feel ugly. Was I a little larger than most girls? Sure, but that didn't bother me. Why should it? I was pretty darn cute, if I did say so myself. And I'd never had a problem getting women into bed, even before BBWs were all the rage, so I clearly wasn't the only one who thought so. I really had no reason to be self-conscious about carrying around a few (dozen) extra pounds.

But with forty now in the rearview mirror I'd started thinking it was time to take better care of myself, get in shape, maybe firm up some of those places that had been squishy for so long.

The insurance company I worked for, in an ongoing effort to promote health and fitness among its employees, sponsored various programs to help us "lose weight, get in shape, stay in shape." Emails about Zumba classes, Turbo Kick classes and seminars on nutrition and weight loss flooded my inbox regularly. It seemed like every day I'd find some exercise-related email taking up some of my digital storage space. Usually I just deleted the emails without even bothering to read them.

But one in particular intrigued me.

Sign Up for Boot Camp Now! the subject line of the latest invasive email shouted at me. *Women-Only Classes Available.*

It wasn't the "women-only" part that got my attention, though that was a definite plus. I didn't have anything against men. Some of my best friends had cocks. But when it came to any kind of workout regiment, I knew I'd be more comfortable if it was just us girls. That wasn't a deal maker, though. It was the boot camp idea that caught my eye. I'd heard of these fitness boot camps. Friends on Facebook mentioned them now and then, and they posted about how much fun they were and the amazing results they got. The email described boot camp as an eight-week program of fun, fitness and motivation. I certainly needed all of those. The class was forty-five dollars and met twice a week (Tuesday and Thursday evenings) in the basement of my office building and I would need to bring an exercise mat. Attached to the email was a pdf file of a registration form.

Boot camp seemed like it would be an interesting experience. The class wasn't very expensive. Having it right there in the office building after work couldn't have been more convenient. I would still have to think about it.

Just in case, I printed off the registration form.

I remembered the newsletter from about a year ago announcing the company had taken a storage room in the basement and converted it into a fitness room for employees to use before and after business hours, but I'd never been down there until the first night of boot camp. It was nice. One half of the room was an open space. Filling the other half were two rows of stationary bikes and treadmills. There was a weight machine in the corner. None were in use. I assumed it was because the room had been reserved for our class. When I got there, a couple of women I really didn't know but had seen around the office had their workout mats spread out on the floor and were chatting with each other. I smiled at them and headed into the changing room, another storage room that had been remodeled the year before. Lockers lined three of the four walls. The fourth was made of mirrors. In front of the lockers were long wooden benches. I found a locker without a lock on it and sat down in front of it.

Since I'd had to go to Target to buy an exercise mat, I'd figured I might as well get some new workout clothes to go with it. I stripped off my work clothes and slipped into a pair of gray sweatpants with blue stripes down the side, a loose-fitting navy T-shirt, and a pair of plain white Chuck Taylors. Then I checked myself out in the mirror. Yep. Pretty darn cute.

A few other women had arrived while I was changing clothes. One of them worked two cubicles down from me and she smiled when she saw me. I waved. I was about to set myself up next to her when our instructor walked in the room.

"Good evening, ladies," the instructor said. "Welcome to boot camp. My name is Kerin, and I'll be busting your butts today."

There was some quiet laughter from the other women, but not from me. I was too stunned to laugh. Or speak. Or think.

Kerin was probably in her early thirties and not very tall. She had short, spiky blonde hair with black roots that reminded me of the guy on "Diners, Drive-Ins, and Dives." She had on a pair of tight black capris and a purple sports bra with a Nike swoosh between her breasts. Her outfit couldn't have been tighter or shown more of her flat tummy. I supposed that was the point.

Was it possible to have negative body fat? I'd never seen anyone so...solid. And I couldn't take my eyes off of her. I think Kerin noticed. She moved to the front of the class and put her hands on her hips.

"I'm glad to see you all here today," she said. "I don't believe in wasting time, so lets get started with some stretches."

Kerin demonstrated what she wanted us to do and the rest of us followed her lead, stretching our legs, arms, backs. I could feel the strain in my muscles as I tried to touch my toes. When was the last time I'd gotten any exercise? I couldn't even remember. Unless really vigorous sex counted. And it should. But even that had been a while.

After the stretching, Kerin had us do some jumping jacks. I hadn't done jumping jacks since high school gym class. That seemed easy enough. But then Kerin added a little twist. After five jumping jacks she had us drop to the floor, do a push-up, jump back to our feet and do five more jumping jacks.

I thought I was going to die.

"Don't worry if you can't do a push-up," Kerin said, weaving her way between us as we jumped, jacked and pushed. "Just do the best you can today and try to do better next time."

The best I could do today was to not have a heart attack. So far I was managing that. But I didn't know how long I could keep it up. After the jumping jacks from hell, Kerin had us doing squat thrusts. I should have enjoyed watching her demonstrate them, but I was dreading doing them too much to really appreciate her demonstration. I tried my best to keep up with everyone but my out-of-shape body was screaming at me to stop.

The five-minute break we got was not enough.

After the break, Kerin had us get flat on our stomachs for an exercise she called the sea turtle. We arched our backs and raised our arms and legs off the floor (which took a lot of effort on its own) then mimicked swimming like a sea turtle. She kept us at it until I thought my arms were going to fall off.

"Great," Kerin said, clapping her hands together. "Since I have you on the floor, I want you to get on your hands and knees. We're going to do some donkey kicks."

I was ready to collapse. What had I gotten myself into?

I thought my body hurt when I got home that night, but it was nothing compared to the ache I felt Wednesday morning when I tried to get out of bed. My body was not happy with me. A long, hot shower and a couple of Advil made the pain manageable enough that I could drag my ass to work, but I was sluggish all day. I felt old. Out of shape. The simple act of taking a few steps seemed to take a lot of effort. And I was going to put myself through this again tomorrow? I didn't think I could even do a single stretch, never mind a squat thrust.

And of course I kept thinking about Kerin in her sports bra and tight black pants. Her body was perfect. Lean, athletic. I couldn't imagine myself doing what it would take to achieve that look. But I could imagine pulling that sports bra up over her head and staring at her naked breasts before I bent down and kissed them. And I could definitely imagine sliding my hand between her legs and rubbing her pussy through the crotch of her capris.

The chance to see Kerin again was worth all the body aches.

The second night of boot camp started out the same as the first, but Kerin tossed a few new exercises at us to keep things interesting. She looked just as amazing as she had two nights before in a nearly identical outfit to the one she'd worn on Tuesday. But I hardly had time to admire her; she kept the pace brisk. It was all I could do to keep up. While I tried to steal glances at her ass when I could, the workout was just too much for me to enjoy looking at her. I did notice that no one else in class seemed to be having as much trouble as I was, even though I wasn't the only big girl there. It was like I was fighting with every exercise. Or more like every exercise was beating up on me and I was just covering my face to protect myself as best I could. Things had to get better, right? If I kept at this, eventually it would have to get easier.

It certainly couldn't get harder.

I thought with several days to recover I'd do better at the next boot camp. And at first that was proving to be true. I stretched, I kicked like a donkey and I crunched my abs. And felt good doing it. But then about twenty minutes in, the ache returned and my arms felt like they weighed a hundred pounds each. Sweat gathered at the small of my back. I just wanted it to be over with. Then Kerin clapped her hands together to get our attention.

"Today we're going to end with something different," she said.

Her words filled me with dread. What now? What book about the Spanish Inquisition had she read over the weekend to inspire her?

"Follow me," Kerin said.

And we did. We followed her out of the room and down the hall. She stopped at the stairwell.

"We're going to work the stairs today," Kerin said. "Up to the fourth floor and back down. This isn't a race, so don't try to make it one. Walking is acceptable. Let's go!"

Kerin took off up the stairs. The rest of the class followed her. I pulled up the rear. Walking may have been acceptable to Kerin, but for me it was mandatory. Run up four flights of stairs? Who the hell was she kidding? I started upstairs and felt like I was wading through four feet of quicksand. But I told myself this was supposed to be good for me, that I would be glad *later* if I did this *now*.

That argument got me to the second floor. Going any farther was out of the question. I sat down on the top step, wanting to cry. Why was I doing this to myself? Was it really worth it? I liked who I was; I was comfortable with how I looked. I didn't need this. What was I trying to prove?

I was still asking myself that in the locker room while I was changing back into my work clothes.

"Are you okay?"

I turned around. Kerin was standing a few feet from me, a concerned look on her face. I was so lost in thought I hadn't even heard the door open behind me. Now I was hyperaware of everything. Like how it was just the two of us in the locker room. And how I hadn't buttoned my blouse yet. If Kerin noticed she didn't let on.

"Feeling my age, but okay," I said.

Kerin smiled. "Good."

"But I don't think I'll be able to finish this class," I said. "It's just too much right now and I'm too out of shape. I thought I could handle it, but I was wrong."

"I think you're doing just fine," Kerin said. "Getting started is the hardest part."

"And quitting is the easiest party," I replied, nodding. "But I think it's for the best."

Kerin shook her head. "I don't believe in giving up. And I don't want to see you give up after three classes. Give it one more chance. And if you still feel this way, then I won't argue."

"I appreciate that," I said. "But I've made up my mind."

Kerin arched an eyebrow at me. "Oh, you have, huh?" She moved closer, close enough that I could feel the heat coming off her body. Though I wouldn't swear I could actually see it, her muscles seemed to be in constant motion, as if the sheath of her skin could barely contain them. She was lightning in a bottle, crackling with energy that needed to escape. I was pretty sure if she didn't work out and expend that energy she would explode. The intensity in her eyes burned into mine and so completely distracted me I didn't notice her hand on the move until it was cupping my breast. Like an idiot, I gasped.

"I think you need some extra-special motivation," Kerin told me softly. She brushed the flat of her thumb over my nipple, teasing it hard through my bra. "I want you to give this class one more chance. Be here on Thursday and I will make it worth your while."

Kerin gave my breast a good, hard squeeze then walked away without another word.

When I got to class on Thursday, Kerin saw me and nodded. "Glad you could make it," she said.

I managed not to blush in front of my coworkers, but I had absolutely no control over the twinge I felt between my legs. Kerin had on the same outfit she'd been wearing the first day of boot camp, and the thought of running my hands over that hard, athletic body she loved showing off made my insides flutter. I just had to make it through this class.

Kerin didn't make it easy.

Once again we started out with stretches. She had us doing push-ups and jumping jacks. We were upright one minute, face down on the floor the next. I was breathless in no time, hurting soon after that. But I thought about Kerin's hand on my breast, and the promise of her touching me other places, and kept going. Even when she led us down the hall and to the stairwell—where I wanted to scream so loud it would echo through the entire building—I just kept going. Up five flights of stairs today and back down, when two days ago I barely made it up one flight. It took me longer than everyone else, and I hurt more than ever, but I still did it.

Everyone else had cleared out by the time I got back to the locker room. I saw no sign of Kerin. My heart sank a little. Had she just been jerking me around? Had I just walked up five flights of stairs and back down again for nothing? I was all geared up to be furious. But then the door opened and Kerin walked in. Everything was quickly forgiven and forgotten.

"Good job today," Kerin said.

I smiled. "Thanks."

"I knew you could do it if you tried."

I didn't know what to say. But I didn't have time to say anything. Kerin closed the distance between us in two quick steps and pinned me against the lockers, her body pressed hard against mine as she kissed me. I grunted against her lips, sliding my hands over her like I had been thinking about since the first time she walked into the fitness room. She was like stone, hard and lean. I could feel the curves of her muscles; feel them moving under her skin, like waves rolling onto the shore. Kerin slid her hand under my T-shirt to grab my breast and I answered her by grabbing her ass with both hands. She moaned and kissed me deeper, her tongue dancing over mine. Once again I was breathless because of her, but for very different reasons this time. Her hand fell away from my breast and moved between my legs. She cupped my mound through my sweats, grinding the heel of her palm into me. I moaned and thrust my hips at her, desperately and pitifully trying to hump her hand.

"Please," I whispered between kisses.

Kissing me again, Kerin shoved her hand down the front of my sweatpants and traced the cleft of my pussy through my

panties. Her touch made me whimper. For the last hour she'd
made my body ache from her sadistic workout routine, and now
my body ached for her touch, ached to have her fingers inside
me. She didn't make me suffer long. Kerin slipped her fingers
under the crotch of my panties and thrust into me, fucking me
so hard I slammed back against the lockers. She pumped her
fingers into my slick cunt, her kisses the only thing keeping my
cries and moans from filling the locker room. My pussy clenched
and unclenched around her fingers in raging fits as she took me
closer and closer to the edge. I could feel my clit pulsing with
need and was desperate for Kerin to touch me there. She had
other plans for me.

Stepping back and pulling me with her, Kerin spun me around
so I was facing the lockers now. She shoved me forward a little
and I groaned when Kerin yanked my sweatpants and panties
down in one fluid motion. I could feel her behind me, feel her
energy, like a wild animal stalking its prey before it strikes. I
hissed through gritted teeth when Kerin slid her hand over my
bare ass and gave it a slap so sharp it echoed through the locker
room like a thunderclap. Then she was inside me again, three
fingers filling my pussy, fucking me from behind. I pushed back
against her, wanting her even deeper inside me, matching each
thrust as Kerin slid her fingers in and out of me. Harder, faster,
deeper. I pressed my cheek against the cool metal of the locker
as Kerin drove me to orgasm. With her fingers inside me, she
reached around with her free hand and attacked my clit from
the front, rubbing it, making little circles around it with the tips
of her first two fingers. I quickly lost it; lost it all over Kerin's
hands. She didn't let up. I rode her fingers until the last ripples
of orgasm faded into stillness.

Struggling to breathe, I turned around to face her. Kerin
stared intently at me, her face flushed, fire burning behind her

hazel eyes. She held up her hand, showed me the fingers she'd had inside me, showed me how they glistened with my juices, and I watched her, transfixed as she wiped my slickness on her bare tummy. Her look turned expectant. She didn't need to say anything. My sweatpants half off me, my insides still quivering, I knelt down in front of Kerin. Her bare midriff with my juices smeared across it was all I could see and I leaned into her, covering her firm tummy with kisses. Kerin moaned above me, her hands tangling in my hair as I kissed and licked her clean, the taste of myself mingled with her sweat making me dizzy. Using both hands, I pulled her capris and her panties down just far enough so I could get at her. The earthy, wet smell of her cunt filled my senses and instead of teasing her like I might have done with another woman, I buried my face in the wetness of her, hungrily lapping at her swollen folds. Kerin tightened her grip in my hair, holding on with both hands as I swirled my tongue inside her. The damp warmth of her pussy covered my face as I ate her, my greedy mouth pressed tight against her hole. I was a woman consumed, possessed. Her moans and sighs sounded faint and distant, barely reaching me in the world I had lost myself in. I slid my hands up the backs of her legs and cupped her tight ass, pulling Kerin onto my face while I fucked her with my tongue. I could feel each spasm of her pussy as I took her to the brink, and when my tongue at last made its way to her swollen clit, those spasms became an earthquake that shook us both to our very core.

After a few seconds of silence, she stroked my hair. "So will I see you in class next week?" Kerin finally asked me.

Breathing in the smell of her, the taste of her on my lips, I turned and leaned my face against the smooth wet heat of Kerin's pussy then whispered, "Yes."

FACING
THE MUSIC

Kiki DeLovely

When Nic suggested we fly out East to attend her twenty-fifth-year high school reunion, I immediately leapt at the opportunity. Although admittedly wary of such events, I couldn't resist the image of us walking into a Catholic school—her, the clean-cut high school jock, with me, a somewhat more colorful, scantily dressed high femme, on her arm—and the ridiculous looks on all her schoolmates' faces that would undoubtedly ensue. It was too good to pass up.

Nic assured me that despite the fact that it was an all-girl institution, we'd be the only queer couple there, but since she was always considered the school's golden girl, we'd easily find folks who were welcoming. What should have put me at ease instead made me increasingly nervous as I got dressed that first night of the event. I had been all riled up about the spectacle aspect of us making an appearance at a very conservative, very Catholic reunion, and once the novelty of that wore off, *entonces qué?* Sure, we'd get some stares, perhaps elicit a whisper or two, but then the open-minded Democrats would take us under their wing and want to reminisce about old times. And I'd die a slow death of boredom. Suddenly I wasn't so excited about the evening ahead, which seemed less and less scandalous by the moment.

We got there a little bit late, so the halls were empty when we walked in, with the faintest sound of '80s music playing in a distant, closed-off space. I could just picture what the room looked like, tackily decorated with streamers, balloons and disco balls. I had been dragging my heels at the hotel—spending way too long deciding what to wear, perfecting my makeup much more so than necessary—anything to delay a night of conversations with a bunch of just-left-of-center old classmates and their partners, I mean husbands. The sound of my heels clicking on the granite echoed down the fluorescent-flickering hallway, brightly colored arrows leading the way toward the reception. Nic had a look on her face I didn't quite recognize, but I could only imagine that all sorts of memories were flooding back, being in this place again after so many years.

Then she took a sharp right unexpectedly and was pulling me down a more dimly lit hallway. "I'm not ready to go in there yet. Let's take you on a tour."

"A tour, huh?" Knowing her as well as I did, I could only imagine what that meant in Nic's beautifully creative mind. But where exactly would she take this? Was she going to pin me up against the head cheerleader's locker? Hoist me onto the art studio's worktables? Perhaps a little naughty schoolgirl play in the science lab? Instead she took me somewhere unexpected...to the locker room. It was clear they hadn't updated this room since the 1940s and yet it was still as pristinely white as I'd imagine it would have been back then. I ran my fingers across the cold, sterilized tiles and tried to picture this room twenty-five years before, filled with girls just out of gym class, my lover in the midst of it all, trying desperately not to stare. As I lost myself in this (somewhat) innocent fantasy, I suddenly found myself pinned up against those same white tiles. The shock of where the cold porcelain met my warm bits of exposed skin made me gasp. My lover covered my mouth quickly with one hand as the other traveled up my inner thigh, trailing slowly, teasing me.

"Don't you dare tell anyone. You got that? I can't have the whole school knowing...." She got me there quickly. I could read her energy and it didn't take much for me to catch up to where her deliciously perverse mind had already taken this. It was like she had just been in my head...and was now taking advantage of an opportunity she saw with the quiet girl. The one who spent too much time in the library, who sat alone in the stands at all the girls' basketball games, who'd never said a word to her favorite player, but she'd caught her staring sometimes. And now that it was my lover, the star player, who'd been caught staring, the quiet girl didn't look away. Finally Nic had found the opportunity to get what she always wanted from this girl.

Once she'd gotten well past the hem of my skirt, yet still an inch or so shy of *mis pantaletas*, I turned to look at her, half-heartedly protesting, "But what about the others?"

"Never you mind them." Her hand paused briefly as she grabbed a healthy handful of my flesh. "The game is over, everyone's showered and gone home by now. I was the last one left. Speaking of, what are you even doing here?" She squeezes that handful of thigh tightly. "You don't belong here."

"I know... *Es que,* well... I was... I was...."

She abruptly cut off my ridiculous stammering, "You were trying to get a peek at me, weren't you?"

The blood pounding in my clit decided to get generous with

my upper half and shot straight up through my veins, defying gravity as it flushed my face. Accused of a crime I knew I'd been guilty of on more than one occasion. *Ay carajo,* there's not enough batting of eyelashes in the universe to blink my way out of this one. Not that I'd want to. I just liked to pretend sometimes. No, right in that second, I was exactly where I wanted to be, ready and willing to face the music. *Así me gusta.*

"Well, now you're gonna get exactly what you've always wanted. Aren't you? This is what you really wanted, isn't it?" And when she didn't get a reply for a second time in a row, she tangled her fist in my hair, pushing my cheek into the wall, repeating more aggressively, "Isn't it!"

My breathing was ragged, condensing along the freshly scrubbed tiles, the caustic scent of Clorox burning my nostrils. In a very small voice I replied, "I've always wanted you."

I have. Even before I met her, I'd dreamt of her. Tall, athletic, short salt-and-pepper hair, the kindest light gray eyes and the dirtiest mind with which I'd ever been graced—Nic knew how to do things to me that even I hadn't yet figured out I wanted. She pressed her weight up against me—sweetly softened in the decades since her sportier days, but lean, hard muscle still very much present underneath it all. In my eyes, she had the ideal physique: pulp and *panza* mixed with sinew and *solidez.*

A split second later, my panties had hit the floor and Nic was gnawing on the side of my neck like a teenage boy. Pushing her hips into my ass, I ground back against her until I couldn't take it any longer. I needed her inside me now. *Dios mío,* I'd never wanted something so bad before in my life. So she spun me around to face her, pressed me back up onto the hard surface, and shoved her fingers in deep. Pumping in and out of me, slowly, purposefully, she drew close to my ear and whispered, "You wanna be my girl?" This unexpected bit of sweetness brought tears to my eyes and I couldn't form any words, so I just nodded, *arroyitos* streaming down my cheeks.

"I've been watching you." The words were barely audible, timidity on my breath. But she was the one watching me now, her gaze intense, and I couldn't bear the weight of it any longer. Reaching out for her bottom lip with my teeth, I took hold of it, sucking and biting down. Nic shoved her tongue in my mouth, wrapping around mine, searching out every last taste bud.

"I go to all of your games," I confessed breathlessly, breaking away and tilting my head back. My vision, watery and out of focus, shifted to the ceiling just briefly before my eyes began rolling back farther. Her thumb circled my clit while she curled her fingers up against my G-spot, working it so fucking good. Relentlessly digging into me. She knew I needed her to keep going. So she fucked me through the tears, until I was squirting all over the pretty white tiles, barely missing her immaculately polished wingtips, begging her not to stop. I moved my hips up and down on her fingers—my body instructing my lover exactly how I needed her thrusting in and out of my dripping cunt.

"I've wanted you for so long." The setting lended itself quite nicely to the scene we'd so easily conjured. These walls housed great memories of her glory days—a time that was now getting the opportunity to be replayed and transformed into something even more truly glorious.

"Nic, oh, yes, Nic...." And as I called out her name, I swore I could hear the voices of her teammates from years past chanting her name. It bounced off all the tiled surfaces, "Nic, Nic, Nic!" Her name echoed through me, resonating with something buried deep inside. She fucked me with so much sweetness, releasing my secrets, bringing all of me to the surface. "Nic, Nic, Nic..." Her name tumbled off my lips like a little prayer and joined the chanting above.

I came fast, unexpectedly, out of nowhere. Her name got stuck in my throat. She curled her arms around me, deftly catching my body as it let go. I got so wrapped up in her—this was where I belonged. In an attempt to even out my breathing, I swallowed hard.

She held me like that for some time and at last my heartbeat began to slow—mine always took longer to mirror hers, no match for the resting heartbeat of a former star athlete. Knowing I'd need to take a few minutes to regain some composure, Nic led me to the sinks, rinsed her hands and left me to reapply my lipstick. To get *bien* pretty, as I like to call it. She paced around, touching everything, the brush of her fingertips across a showerhead imbuing a flood of memories. It was as if she could invoke the good ol' days just by grounding herself in this place.

I turned away from the mirror and took a few steps to her before she stopped me. "Wait."

I looked back at my reflection self-consciously. "What is it?" I tousled my hair.

"You look like an angel. I want to remember this exact moment. I love having you here. Back then I could've never imagined such a future for myself. Now you're a part of what that chapter of my life meant to me."

I smiled and cocked my head, taking all of her in as her eyes devoured me. Then, at the same moment, we both set time back into motion and made our way out, readying ourselves for the big public appearance.

Nic opened the door for me and gliding past her, I demurely asked, "So, Number Sixty-Five, you got a date for the dance?"

"Yes. Yes, I most definitely do." And with that, she took my hand, twirling me out, spinning me back into her over and over again until we reached the doors of the grand hall. We could hear Heart piping through the speakers: *Cause there's the girl that you were after/Feel your heart beating faster now.* Nic offered her arm to me and I took a deep breath as I placed my hand a bit higher than normal, curling my fingers around her delicious bicep—even more greatly defined than when she originally roamed these halls. After our locker room escapade, I was ready to face just about anything...even cheesy '80s music.

OUT AND
A BOUT

Allison Wonderland

Y ou're not skating on thin ice, Val. You're going to be fine."

Claudia's at the brink of the rink, arms draped over the wall, body bent at the waist with her rump sticking out as if she's waiting for a spanking. I ought to strike some fear into her. She did the same to me and I didn't even get a spanking.

Claud winks at me. I glare at her. She's so confident and cavalier and superbly sexy and inevitably the glaring turns to staring and I still want to spank her, but for all the wrong reasons.

"Come on, Val," she urges. She skates onto the carpet and stops in front of me. "Get your butt in gear."

"There's no protective gear to get my butt in," I lament, adjusting the Velcro on the kneepads Claud lent me. I hate that ripping sound it makes. It's so ominous. "Forget it. I'm not skating. I'm on the bench."

"I can see that," Claud quips, dropping down onto the stiff wooden seat. She picks up the helmet. It looks like an eight ball and feels like a salad bowl. My curls are crushed. Claudia fastens the straps, her knuckles nuzzling my chin. I don't mind this part so much.

Claud knows it, too, flashing her little snowman smile at me. She lifts my leg onto her lap. My calf gyrates against her thigh as she laces up the skates. I don't mind this part so much, either. Nevertheless, I say, "I've already fallen for you, Claudia. Why do I have to do it again?"

Claud rubs my leg. It feels nice, but not as nice as it feels when I touch hers. She's much more robust than I am. Whereas Claud is a cross between Wonder Woman and Rosie the Riveter, I've got the body of a stick-figure drawing. Anyway, "Who says you're going to fall?" she challenges.

"It's a given."

"I knew you'd give in," Claud crows. "That's why I didn't give up." She taps the cap of my kneepad. I do the same.

"Ouch."

"Don't be such a sissy, missy. A little pain never hurt anyone."

"Who are you?"

"I'm your number one," Claud answers. "And you're my number one fan. Or you will be after the bout tonight." She stands, takes my left hand. I've got a wrist pad on the right one, so maybe I won't break *every* bone in my body.

"No, I mean, what's your derby name?"

"Lisa *Welt-chel*," she answers, hoisting me onto my skates. The wheels are orange like a basketball and clash with the camel-colored boots. But these boots aren't made for walking and I practically pulverize Claudia's hand as I wobble across the carpet. "Most players pick names that pay homage to inspiring women," Claud continues, unfazed. "Mine pays homage to Lisa Whelchel."

"The lady who played Blair Warner is inspiring?"

"When I was fourteen, she inspired my latent lesbian libido,"

Claudia shares. "I'd watch the show on Nick at Nite and all these impure thoughts would pop into my head. She forced me to face the facts."

I'd roll my eyes except I'm too focused on rolling my wheels, four of which are now in the rink. *Please, God, don't let me die with my boots on. Not when they're this tacky. Just help me bumble and fumble and, if I have to, tumble my way through this. But please keep in mind that I bruise easily. And also that—*

"Come on, Val," Claud cuts in. "Let's get these wheels in motion." She pulls on my arm as if it's a rope in a tug-of-war game.

Instinctively, I utter a corny exclamation—"Yikes!"—and thrust both toe stops against the wood floor. This has the undesired effect of throwing me even more off balance.

"You look like a bombed ballerina," Claud titters while I totter. "You need to relax," she urges, steadying me. "Just let go and hold on."

It's surprisingly good advice, and before long, I'm gliding glacially and (sort of) gracefully around the rink. Not exactly hell on wheels, but who gives a hoot? Once I stop focusing so much on my feet, I start to survey my surroundings. The rink is like a disco, a warehouse, and our solar system, all rolled into one. It's actually a pretty neat place, although I'd probably feel differently if the space were jam-packed. Claud had the good sense to bring me here on a Saturday morning.

She thinks that if I just put myself in her shoes—well, skates— I'll feel more comfortable with what she does. But I'm not sure I can embrace a sport whose players are cruising for a bruising. My idea of a contact sport is thumb wrestling, and even that's too dangerous for me. Okay, so I'm tame. And lame. I know it. Sex, hugs, and rock 'n' roll—that's about all I can handle. And possibly Ping-Pong, but even that sport has its hazards.

I'm not like Claudia. Claudia's got moxie and mettle and a

high tolerance for pain. Sure, I like a light spanking every once
in a while, but the derby is different. It's…brutal. And contu-
sions are not confined to a single area of the body. As much as I
love making love with Claudia, and even though she brags about
her bruises, it still pains me to look at them—which is why I've
avoided going to her games. I can't do that anymore, though,
not since Claud decided that my I'll-be-there-in-spirit support
is no longer sufficient. So, to commemorate our six months of
togetherness, I've agreed to attend tonight's bout.

"You're on a roll," Claud comments, squeezing my hand. It's
refreshing, being able to hold hands in public, even if it's more
of a safety measure than a display of affection. It still counts. I
smile at our joined hands. My grip has loosened somewhat, so
Claud's skin has returned to its natural color: golden-brown, like
a sugar cone. It looks neat with her nails, painted unicorn-white
and speckled with electric-blue dots. One of her rings is blue,
too. It's a friendship ring, and Claud's sporting a rainbow of
these braided neon bands, all from her teammates. The Curious
George Band-Aid is from me—I put it on after she sustained a
paper cut from the Victoria's Secret catalogue.

Claudia squeezes my hand again, her fingers firm against my
flesh. I love her hand holding mine. Her fingers are long and
lithe and I like the way her rings and things tickle my skin. I like
the pressure of her palm, too, and the bend of her bones against
my own. I like the way—

"Hey! Claudia, come back here!"

Claudia has released my hand and started skating away. I tilt
one foot until the toe stop sits atop the wood floor. A few paces
ahead, Claud pauses, whips around and holds her arms out.
"Come on, Val," she urges. "Come to me, come on."

The distance is discouraging. "How am I supposed to get
from here to there?"

"Skate," she states, as if it's painfully obvious, which it will be when I fall on my butt. "You can do it, Val. I have complete faith in you." She stretches her arms toward me. "Come on, Val, come on," Claud coos, like a mother encouraging her toddler to walk independently for the very first time. Scowling, I force one foot in front of the other. "Atta girl. That's it. Almost there, almost there," Claud continues, as if she's coaxing me to orgasm.

It's one of those thoughts that you think without thinking and I stumble slightly. But I don't lose my footing. In fact—

"You did it!" Claud cheers, pulling me the rest of the way into her arms. She spins me around and I have no choice but to glom on to her like a mollusk. "Now we're roll mates," she announces. "Soul mates on wheels." The hurling hug goes on hiatus, much to my relief. "You were stupendous, by the way. I'm so proud of you."

Claud kisses me. It's hard but soft and it's a good thing she's still holding me because her kisses tend to make me a little unsteady on my feet.

"Yeah, well, you're a good roll model."

"Where do you want me?"

"In my arms," Claudia answers, reaching for my waist.

"No, I mean, where should I sit?" I clarify, but I don't push her away, even though we're in public. A bunch of booths are set up around the field house: artisans, merchandise vendors, groups advocating for the rights of the LGBT community. So I doubt this is a place where patrons take issue with gay PDA.

"Sit in the suicide seats," Claud suggests, returning my attention to the flat track in front of us. "I'll come flying around, land right in your lap. Wham, bam—"

"No thank you, ma'am."

Claud chuckles, but she looks a little disappointed, as if there really is such a thing as suicide seats.

"See those people sitting on the floor?" Claud points to a cluster of fans seated about ten feet away from the track.

"Why would they want to sit that close? They must be suicidal."

"That's why they're in the suicide seats."

"Where are the I-want-to-live seats?" I inquire, scanning the field house.

Claud takes my hand, leads me to the last row of folding chairs in a much safer seating area.

"Will I still be able to see you?"

"In bits and pieces," Claud giggles. I glower. "Sit. I'm going to go put my uniform on."

While Claudia changes in the locker room, I mentally prepare myself for the impending bout. Truth be told, I'm kind of pumped. Petrified, sure, but pumped nonetheless. I put my jacket on an empty chair to claim it, and then, just out of curiosity, I sneak back over to the su...the rink-side seats. The floor is hard and hardly comfortable, but that doesn't matter, because the relocation is only temporary.

The other team is warming up. Well, one of the other teams—Claud says it's a double header. There's nothing scary going on yet. A little pushing and shoving, but nothing I can't handle. I wonder which one of these players is the fastest, the strongest, the nicest, the meanest... I'm telling you, if one of these ladies dares to hurt mine, I'll...try not to let it bother me. I can do that. Yeah, I can grin and bear it, put on a happy—

"Happy anniversary!"

Claudia is barreling toward me. Instinctively, I utter a corny exclamation—"Eep!"—and slam my eyes shut. I hear shrieking and the skidding of skates and then she hits the floor.

"Relax," Claudia says after the fact. "I took a crash course in crashing."

I open my eyes again. Claudia is in my lap, one leg wedged beneath my thigh, the other lounging in my lap. It looks like we're scissoring.

Claud grins, readjusts her helmet. She's wearing her uniform now: Tin Man–silver shorts and a dove-colored tank top. *Starlight Express* meets *Xanadu*. It's practical, though, if not carefully calculated to show off her clout and her curves.

"It's my turn to warm up."

I didn't wait *my* turn to warm up. "Break a...uh...um, drive safely?" Jeez, I didn't mean to get so het up over that getup.

Claudia gets to her feet and takes me with her. "See you during halftime," she chuckles, and pecks my cheek. "Enjoy!"

Before retreating to my seat, I order lemonade from the concession stand, and by the time the bout begins, I'm no longer in a jam, although Claudia is. That's what's supposed to happen, she says—if I remember correctly, each thirty-minute play period consists of two-minute jams, during which the skaters score points. Claud's a blocker, which I guess means she's supposed to block her...and her...and, yeah, the rest of the details are kind of fuzzy. But Claud's glowing, so either she's having a blast or her team is doing great. From the looks of the scoreboard, both assessments are accurate.

I try to relax and enjoy. The game is so theatrical. The choreography is amazing—the way the pack of players careens around the track like a human roller coaster. After ten minutes, I'm cheering for Claud, not fearing for her.

I want a better view. I want to be able to keep track of Claudia. I move out of my seat and into one that's closer.

God, she looks beautiful out there, all nerve and verve, hustle and muscle. I can see why she likes this sport so much—it promotes agility over fragility, demands physical strength and strength of character. I love the way her body moves: wending and bending and sending her opponents offtrack.

But it's not brutal. It's...hot.

Claudia's movements may be propelling her around the track, but they're also impelling my one-track mind, and by halftime, I'm half crazed with longing.

"What do you think?" Claudia asks, draping her arm across my shoulders. She's panting and perspiring. That makes two of us.

"You're doing a bang-up job," I answer, clapping her on the backside.

Claud blushes a bit. "Thanks." She removes one wrist pad and takes my cup of lemonade.

"I can think of better ways to swap spit," I remark as she pokes the straw between her lips.

Claud's eyebrows head toward her helmet. "Are you okay, Val?"

My fingers make their way under Claud's tank top and crawl up her back, as if she's a hand puppet. "I'm a little...libidinous."

This cracks Claud up. "I blame myself. I'm the one who told you to enjoy the game. I probably should have set some limits on that, huh?"

My gaze zips around the field house. Where can we...? There! An abandoned booth. One of the vendors didn't show, I guess. The booth is pushed up against a wall and dressed in a long, purple table skirt. "Perfect!"

I grab Claud's hand. She has to speed skate just to keep up with me. "You're no sissy, missy," she murmurs as I pull her inside our frilly fort.

My body is a spiral of sensations, lust whooshing and whipping and whooping it up. I shove my hand into her shorts, head straight for her cunt.

"You're rough," she says, as my fingers collide with her clit.

"That's tough," I say, though it sounded more like a compliment than a complaint.

Claud rips my zipper open, jams her hand inside my jeans.

The combustion continues, intensifies, until we're reduced to smashing lips and thrashing hips.

"I'm really glad I came." Claudia giggles. I do the same. "To the game," I clarify, and we giggle some more.

Claud taps the cap of her kneepad, leaving behind a damp dot. "What was that all about, anyway?"

I finger the straps of her helmet. "Your wheels were spinning," I answer, my knuckles nuzzling her chin, "and so were mine."

THE OUTSIDE EDGE

Sacchi Green

Suli was fire and wine, gold and scarlet, lighting up the dim passageway where we waited.

I leaned closer to adjust her Spanish tortoiseshell comb. A cascade of dark curls brushed my face, shooting sparks all the way down to my toes, but even a swift, tender kiss on her neck would be too risky. I might not be able to resist pressing hard enough to leave a dramatic visual effect the TV cameras couldn't miss.

Tenderness wasn't what she needed right now and neither was passion. An edgy outlet for nervous energy would be more like it. "Skate a clean program," I murmured in her ear, "and maybe I'll let you get dirty tonight." My arm across her shoulders might have looked locker-room casual, but the look she shot me had nothing to do with team spirit.

"*Maybe*, Jude? You think maybe you'll *let* me?" She tossed her head. Smoldering eyes, made even brighter and larger by theatrical makeup, told me that I'd need to eat my words later before my mouth could move on to anything more appealing.

The other pairs were already warming up. Suli followed Tim into the arena, her short scarlet skirt flipping up oh-so-accidentally to reveal her firm, sweet ass. She wriggled, daring me to give it an encouraging slap, knowing all too well what the rear view of a scantily clad girl does for me.

I moved into the stadium and watched the action from just outside the barrier. As Suli and Tim moved onto the ice, the general uproar intensified. Their groupies had staked a claim near one end, and a small cadre of my own fans were camped out nearby, having figured out over the competition season that something was up between us. Either they'd done some discreet stalking or relied on the same gaydar that had told them so much about me even before I'd fully understood it myself. Probably both.

Being gay wasn't, in itself, a career-buster these days. Sure, the rumormongers were eternally speculating about the men in their sequined outfits, but the skating community was united in a compact never to tell, and the media agreed tacitly never to ask. A rumor of girl-on-girl sex would probably do nothing more than inspire some fan fiction in certain blogging communities. That didn't mean there weren't still lines you couldn't cross in public, especially in performance—lines I was determined, with increasing urgency, to cross once and for all.

But I didn't want to bring Suli down if I fell. That discussion was something we kept avoiding, and whenever I tried to edge toward it she'd distract me in ways I couldn't resist.

Suli's the best, I thought now in the stadium, watching her practice faultless jumps with Tim. You'd never guess what she'd been doing last night with me, while the other skaters were preparing for the performance of their lives with more restful rituals. She'd already set records in pairs skating, and next year, at my urging, she was going to go solo. It was a good thing I wouldn't be competing against her.

I won't be competing against anybody, I thought, my mind wandering as the warm-up period dragged on.

It had taken me long enough to work it out, focusing on my skating for so many years, but the more I appreciated the female curves inside those scanty, seductive costumes, the less comfortable I was wearing them. Cute girls in skimpy outfits were just fine with me—bodies arched in laybacks, or racing backward, glutes tensed and pumping, filmy fabric fluttering in the breeze like flower petals waving to the hungry bees—but I'd rather see than be one.

I'd have quit mainstream competition if they hadn't changed the rules to allow long-legged "unitards" instead of dresses. That concession wasn't enough to make me feel really comfortable, though, and I knew my coach was right that some judges would hold it against me if I didn't wear a skirt at least once in a while. This year I'd alternated animal-striped unitards with a Scottish outfit just long enough to preserve the mystery of what a Scotsman wears under his kilt, assuming that he isn't doing much in the way of spins or jumps or spirals. I knew this for certain, having experimented in solitary practice with my own sturdy six inches of silicone pride.

So why not just switch to the Gay Games? Or follow Rudy Galindo and Surya Bonaly to guest appearances on SkateOut's "Cabaret on Ice"?

If you have a shot at the Olympics, the Olympics are where you go, that's why. Or so I'd thought. But I was only in fifth place after the short program—maybe one or two of the judges weren't that keen on bagpipe music—and a medal was too long a shot now.

I knew, deep down, what the problem was. Johanna, the coach we shared, had urged me to study Suli's style in hopes that some notion of elegance and grace might sink into my thick head. Suli had generously agreed to try to give me at least a trace of an artistic clue. But the closer we became, the more I'd rebelled against faking a feminine grace and elegance that were so naturally hers, and so unnatural for me.

This would be my last competition, no matter what. Maybe I'd get a pro gig with a major ice show, maybe I wouldn't. If I did, it would be on my own terms. "As God is my witness, I'll never be girlie again!" I'd proclaimed melodramatically to Suli last night.

"Works just fine for me," she'd said, kneeling with serene poise to take my experimental six inches between her glossy, carmined lips and deep into her velvet throat.

Ten minutes later, serenity long gone, I stood braced against the edge of the bed and bore her weight while she clamped her thighs around my hips and her cunt around my pride, locked her hands behind my neck and rode me with fierce, pounding joy. I dug my fingers into her asscheeks to steady her and to add to the driving force of her lunges. Small naked breasts slapped against mine on each forward stroke. When I could catch one succulent nipple in my mouth her cries would rise to a shriller pitch, but then she'd jerk roughly away to get more leverage for each thrust.

My body ached with strain and arousal and the friction of the harness. My mind was a blur of fantasies. *We're whirling in the arena, my skates carving spirals into the ice, her dark hair lifting in the wind...*

"Spin me!" Suli suddenly arched her upper body into a layback position, arms no longer gripping me but raised into a pleading curve. Adrenaline, muscles, willpower; none of it was enough now. Only speed could keep us balanced. I stepped back from the bed and spun in place, swinging her in one wide circle, then another, tension hammering through my clit hard enough to counter the burn of the leather gouging my flesh.

Suli's voice whipped around us, streaming as free as her hair. I held on, battling gravity, riding the waves of her cries, until, as they crested, the grip of her legs around me began to slip. In two lurching steps I had her above the bed again, and in another second she was on the sheets. I pressed on until her breathing began to slow, then covered her tender breasts and mouth with a storm of kisses close to bites until I had to arch my back and pump and grind my way to a noisy release of my own.

When we'd sprawled together in delirious exhaustion long enough for our panting to ease, I raised up to gaze at her. The world-famous princess of poise and grace lay tangled in her own wild hair, lips swollen, skin streaked with sweat and most likely bruised in places where the TV cameras had better not reach.

"And *you* lectured *me* about never jumping without knowing exactly where I was going to land!" I said. "How did you know I wouldn't drop you?"

"Aren't you always bugging me to let you try lifts?" she countered drowsily. "You've spun me before, on the ice; you're tall and strong enough." She rolled over on top of me and murmured into the hollow of my throat, "Anyway, I did know where I was going to land. And I knew that you'd get me there. You always do." Then her head slumped onto my shoulder and her body slid down to nestle in the protective curve of mine. In seconds she was asleep.

I always will, I mouthed silently, but couldn't say it aloud. Giving way to tenderness, to emotions deeper than the pyro-technics of sex, was more risk than I could handle. Wherever I was going to land, she belonged somewhere better. *How am I going to bear it? How can we still be together?*

* * *

I shook my head to clear it. Suli and Tim were gliding with the
rest of the competitors toward the edge of the ice and I realized
suddenly that it was time to take my seat in the stands. The final
grouping of the pairs long program was about to get underway.

Suli and Tim skated third, to music from Bizet's *Carmen*.
Somebody always skates to *Carmen,* but no one ever played the
part better than Suli. The dramatic theme of love and betrayal
was a perfect setting for her, and today the passionate beat of
the "Habanera" was a perfect match for my jealous mood.

Watching Tim with Suli on the ice always drove me crazy.
When his hand slid from the small of her back to her hip I
wanted to lunge and chew it off at the wrist. His boyfriend Thor,
a speed skater with massively muscled thighs, would have been
highly displeased by that, so it was just as well that I resisted
the impulse.

It wasn't really the way Tim touched Suli that burned me.
Well, okay, maybe it was, with every nuance of the traditional
lifts and holds pulsing with erotic innuendo. Still, my hands
knew her needs far better than he ever could, or cared to. But he
was allowed to do it publicly, artistically, acting out scenarios of
fiery love—and I wasn't. Knowing that the delectable asscheeks
filling the taut scarlet seat of her costume bore bruises in the
shapes of my fingers was only small comfort.

His other hand rested lightly on her waist as they whirled
across the ice. Any second—in six more beats—she would jump,
and with simultaneous precision he would lift, and throw...
Now! For all the times I'd seen it, my breath still caught. Suli
twisted impossibly high into the air, and far out...out...across
the ice.

Yes! Throw triple axel! A perfect one-footed landing flowing
into a smooth, graceful follow-through, then up into a double

loop side by side with Tim in clockwork synchronicity.

It was the best. The audience knew it; the judges knew it. I knew it, and admiration nearly won out over envy when Tim lifted Suli high overhead, her legs spread wide, in the ultimate hand-in-crotch position known as the Helicopter. Envy surged back. Her crotch would be damp with sweat and excitement, not the kind I could draw from her, but still! Then she dropped abruptly past his face, thighs briefly scissoring his neck, pussy nudging his chin. I shook, nearly whimpering, as Suli slid sensuously down along Tim's body. As soon as her blades touched down she leaned back, back, impossibly far back, until her hair brushed the ice in a death spiral. I tensed as though my hand, not Tim's, gripped hers to brace her just this side of disaster.

A few judges always took points off for "suggestive" material. What did they think pairs skating was all about, if not sex? But it was a technically clean and ambitious program, beautifully executed. Suli and Tim won the gold medals they deserved.

I got no chance to go for the gold of Suli's warm body that night. When I came up behind her in our room and reached around to cup her breasts, she wriggled her compact butt against me, then turned and shoved me away.

"No," she decreed, putting a finger across my lips as I tried to speak. I nibbled at it instead. "You have your long program tomorrow, and I know better than you do what you need."

I tried to object, with no luck.

"Sure," Suli went on, "fast and furious sex and complete exhaustion were just what I needed, but you'll do better saving up that energy and channeling the tension into your skating."

"It doesn't matter," I said sulkily. "I can't medal now anyway. I was thinking, in fact, that this might as well be the time..."

She knew what I meant. "No!" Her scowl was at least as alluring as her smiles. "You can still win the bronze, if you want it enough. At least two of those prima donnas ahead of you have never skated a clean long program in their lives. Medal, and you get into the exhibition at the end. That's the time to make your grand statement to the world." She saw my hesitation and gripped my shoulders so hard her nails dug in. "Think of Johanna! You can't disgrace your coach during actual competition. And think of your fans!" Her expression eased into a smile she couldn't suppress. Her grip eased. "Okay, your fans would love every minute of it. I've seen the signs they flip at you when they're sure the cameras can't see. 'We Want Jude, Preferably in the Nude!'" She drew her fingers lightly across my chest and downward. "Can't say that I blame them."

Suli was so close that her warm scent tantalized me. I thought I was going to get some after all, but the kiss I grabbed was broken off all too soon, leaving me aching for more.

"Please Jude, do it this way." She stroked my face, brushing back my short, dark hair. I wasn't sure I could bear her gentleness. "Even your planned routine comes close enough to the edge. One way or another, it will be worth it. I promise."

So I did it her way, and skated the long program I'd rehearsed so many times. Inside, though, I was doing it my way at last, and not much caring if it showed.

I skated to a medley from the Broadway show *Cats*. My black unitard with white down the front and at the cuffs was supposed to suggest a "tuxedo" cat with white paws. The music swept from mood to mood, poignance to nostalgia to swagger, but no matter what character a song was meant to suggest, in my mind and gut I was never, for a moment, anybody's sweet pussy. I was every inch a Tom. Tomcat prowling urban roofs and alleys; tomboy tumbling the dairymaid in the hay; top-hatted Tom in the back streets of Victorian London pinching the housemaids' cheeks, fore and aft.

Suli had been right about storing up tension and then letting it spill out. Like fantasy during sex, imagination sharpened my performance. Each move was linked to its own notes of the music, practiced often enough to be automatic, but tonight my footwork was more precise, my spins faster, my jumps higher and landings smoother. I had two quad jumps planned, something none of my rivals would attempt, and for the first time I went into each of them with utter confidence.

The audience, subdued at first, was with me before the end, clapping, stomping, whistling. I rode their cheers, pumped with adrenaline as though we were all racing toward some simultaneous climax, and in the last minute I turned a planned double-flip, double-toe-loop into a triple-triple, holding my landing on a back outer edge as steadily as though my legs were fresh and rested.

The crowd's roar surged as the music ended. Fans leaned above the barrier to toss stuffed animals, mostly cats, onto the ice, and one odd flutter caught my eye in time for a detour to scoop up the offering. Sure enough, the fabric around the plush kitten's neck was no ribbon, but a pair of lavender panties. Still warm. It wasn't the first time.

Suli waited at the gate. I gave her a cocky grin and thrust the toy into her hands. Her expressive eyebrows arched higher, and then she grinned back and swatted my butt with it.

The scoring seemed to take forever. "Half of them are scrambling to figure out if you've broken any actual rules," Johanna muttered, "and scheming to make up some new ones if you haven't." The rest, though, must have given me everything they had. The totals were high enough to get me the bronze medal, even when none of the following skaters quite fell down.

Suli stuck by me every minute except for the actual awards ceremony, and she was right at the front of the crowd then. In the cluster of fans following me out of the arena, a few distinctly catlike "Mrowrr's!" could be heard, and then good-humored laughter as Suli threw an arm around me and aimed a ferocious "Growrr!" back over her shoulder at them.

Medaling as a long shot had condemned me to a TV interview. The reporter kept her comments to the usual inanities, except for a somewhat suggestive, "That was quite some program!"

"If you liked that, don't miss the exhibition tomorrow," I said to her, and to whatever segment of the world watches these things. When I added that I was quitting competition to pursue my own "artistic goals," she flashed her white teeth and wished me luck, and then, microphone set aside and camera off, leaned close for a moment to lay a hand on my arm. "Nice costume, but I'll bet you'll be glad to get it off."

Suli was right on it, her own sharp teeth flashing and her long nails digging into my sleeve. The reporter snatched her hand back just in time. "Don't worry," Suli purred, "I've got all that covered."

Don't expose yourself like that! Don't let me drag you down! But I couldn't say it, and I knew Suli was in no mood to listen.

I was too tired, anyway, wanting nothing more than to strip off the unitard and never squirm into one again, but Suli wouldn't let me change in the locker room. Once I saw the gleam of metal she flashed in her open shoulder bag—so much for security at the Games!—I followed her out and back to our room with no regret for the parties we were missing.

The instant the door clicked shut behind us she had the knife all the way out of its leather sheath. "Take off that medal," she growled, doing a knockout job of sounding menacing. "The rest is mine."

I set the bronze medal on the bedside table, flopped backward onto the bed and spread my arms and legs wide. "Use it or lose it," I said, then gasped at the touch of the hilt against my throat.

"Don't move," she ordered, crouching over me, her hair brushing my chest. I lay frozen, not a muscle twitching, although my flesh shrank reflexively from the cold blade when she sat back on her haunches and slit the stretchy unitard at the juncture of thigh and crotch.

"Been sweating, haven't we?" she crooned, slicing away until the fabric gaped like a hungry mouth, showing my skin pale beneath. "But it's not all sweat, is it?" Her cool hand slid inside to fondle my slippery folds. It certainly wasn't all sweat.

Her moves were a blend of ritual and raw sex. The steel flat against my inner thigh sent tongues of icy flame stabbing deep into my cunt. The keen edge drawn along my belly and breastbone seemed to split my old body and release a new one, though only a few light pricks drew blood. The rip of the fabric parting under Suli's knife and hands and, eventually, teeth, was like the rending of bonds that had confined me all my life.

Then Suli's warm mouth captured my clit. The trancelike ritual vanished abruptly in a fierce, urgent wave of right here, right now, right *NOW NOW NO-O-W-W-W-W!* Followed, with hardly a pause to recharge, by further waves impelled by her teasing tongue and penetrating fingers until I was completely out of breath and wrung out.

"I thought I was supposed to be storing up energy," I told her, when I could talk at all.

"Jude, you're pumping out enough pheromones to melt ice," Suli said, "and I'm not ice!"

It turned out that I wasn't all that wrung out, after all, and if I couldn't talk, it was only because Suli was straddling my face, and my mouth was most gloriously, and busily, full.

The chill kiss of the blade lingered on my skin the next day, along with the heat of Suli's touch. I passed up the chance to do a run-through of my program, which didn't cause much comment since it was just the exhibition skate. Johanna, who knew what I was up to, took care of getting my music to the sound technicians with no questions asked.

There were plenty of questioning looks, though, when I went through warm-up muffled in sweats and a lightweight hoodie. Judging from the buzz among my fans, they may have been placing bets. Anybody who'd predicted the close-cropped hair with just enough forelock to push casually back, and the unseen binding beneath my plain white T-shirt, would have won. The tight blue jeans looked genuinely worn and faded, and from any distance the fact that the fabric could stretch enough for acrobatic movement wasn't obvious.

It was my turn at last. Off came the sweats and hoodie. I took to the ice, rocketing from shadows into brightness, then stopped so abruptly that ice chips erupted around the toes of my skates. There were squeals and confused murmurs; I was aware of Suli, still in costume from her own performance, watching from the front row.

Then my music took hold.

Six bars of introduction, a sequence of strides and glides—and I was Elvis, "Lookin' for Trouble," leaping high in a spread eagle, landing, then twisting into a triple-flip, double-toe-loop. My body felt strong. And free. And *true.*

Then I was "All Shook Up," laying a trail of intricate footwork the whole length of the rink, tossing in enough cocky body-work to raise an uproar. Elvis Stojko or Philippe Candeloro couldn't have projected more studly appeal. When my hips swiveled—with no trace of a feminine sway—my fans went wild.

They subsided as the music slowed to a different beat, slower, menacing. "Mack the Knife" was back in town: challenge, swagger, jumps that ate up altitude, skate blades slicing the ice in sure, rock-steady landings. Then, in a final change of mood, came the aching, soaring passion of "Unchained Melody." I let heartbreak show through, loneliness, sorrow, desperate longing.

In my fantasy a slender, long-haired figure skated in the shadows just beyond my vision, mirroring my moves with equal passion and unsurpassable grace. Through the haunting strains of music I heard the indrawn breaths of a thousand spectators, and then a vast communal sigh. I was drawing them into my world, making them see what I imagined... I jumped, pushing off with all my new strength, spun a triple out into an almost effortless quad, landed—and saw what they had actually seen.

Suli glided toward me, arms outstretched, eyes wide and bright with challenge. I stopped so suddenly I would have fallen if my hands hadn't reached out reflexively to grasp hers. She moved backward, pulling me toward her, and then we were skating together as we had so often in our private predawn practice sessions. The music caught us, melded us into a pair. Suli moved away, rotated into an exquisite layback spin, slowed, stretched out her hand, and my hand was there to grasp hers and pull her into a close embrace. Her raised knee pressed up between my legs with a force she would never have exerted on Tim. I wasn't packing, but my clit lurched with such intensity that I imagined it bursting through my jeans.

Then we moved apart again, aching for the lost warmth, circling, now closer, now farther...the music would end so soon... Suli flashed a quick look of warning, mouthed silently, "Get ready!" and launched herself toward me.

Hands on my shoulders, she pushed off, leapt upward, and hung there for a moment while I gripped her hips and pressed my mouth into her belly. Then she wrapped her legs around my waist and arched back. We spun slowly, yearningly, no bed, this time, to take the weight of our hunger. And then, as the last few bars of music swelled around us, Suli slid sensuously down my body until she knelt in a pool of scarlet silk at my feet. She looked up into my eyes, and finally, gracefully and deliberately, bowed her head and rested it firmly against my crotch as the last notes faded away.

An instant of silence, of stillness, followed, until the crowd erupted in chaos, cheers and applause mingling with confusion and outrage. TV cameras were already converging on our exit. I pulled Suli up so that my mouth was close to her ear; her hair brushing my cheek still made me tingle.

"Suli, what have you done? What will—?"

She shushed me with a finger across my lips. "Sometimes, if you can't stand to be left behind, you *do* have to jump without knowing exactly where you'll land."

So I kissed her right there on the ice for the world to see. Then, hand in hand, we skated toward the gate to whatever lay beyond.

HAIL MARY

Shanna Germain

Love

I know it's her by the back of her neck. Something so simple—
the curved pale length of her neck as she shifts her head—and
I know without a doubt that it's Mary. Her hair is darker now,
more gold and less pale blonde, and shorter too, cut in tight
curls that stick close to her head. She's writing on something
behind the counter, her back to us. As thin as she always was,
boyish with just a swell of hips inside her dark jeans. My heart
lobs its aching beat into my throat. At the same time, the pulse
between my legs beats so hard and fast I can feel it all the way
up my stomach.

I stand, frozen. For a moment, I think I can turn and walk
away. I can pretend I never saw her. I can pretend I was never
here.

"Mom…" My daughter, Elsie, tugs my sleeve, her voice full
of awe, and pulls me toward the wall of racquets. She's fifteen

and just made the school tennis team. All week she's talked of nothing but getting her own racquet, her own set of neon-green balls, to practice and play with.

The woman behind the counter, the one that I know is Mary, turns at the sound of my daughter's voice, her smile the kind that's for customers, especially ones that have been accidentally ignored. Her V-necked T-shirt is icy blue; the color makes her eyes glow in the pale heart of her face. She sees me and opens her mouth, her soft pink lips parted slightly, but she doesn't speak. There is a silence, one of those that feels like forever, and then as soon as it's over, you know it was only a second, half a second, tops. Heat slides up through my face. I can feel the prickle in my cheeks and my forehead.

"Mom," Elsie says again, her voice reminding me: fifteen, tennis team, new racquet. The rules of decorum and polite society can hardly be expected to apply to her at this moment.

"Go ahead and look." I try to pretend my mouth hasn't lost all its feeling, all its ability to do the work of talking to my daughter. "See which ones you like."

Elsie bounds off. Endless energy, long legs, her blonde pony-tail flipping behind her. Mary and I both watch her go.

"Well. Maggie-May," Mary says, once Elsie is fondling racquets and racquet strings off in the corner. Mary leans her elbows on the counter, cants her body toward me, her smile big and a little off center. The years have carved small wrinkles at the corners of her mouth, more on one side than the other. There's a black design inked along the inside of her wrist. It looks like a word. "Holy fucking shit," she says.

I laugh, even though that's the last thing I expect to do. No one's called me Maggie-May since Mary. No one says "holy fucking shit" like she does, either, like it's all one word. Prob-ably no one ever will.

"Yeah, holy fucking shit." I can't remember the last time I had those kinds of swear words in my mouth, and it feels good to say them. I push my hair back off my shoulder—it's long now, darkened even more by time and a good colorist—but now it feels too long for my age. Too wild and needy.

"And a daughter?" Mary asks.

"Yeah." I wish I could find another word, or another rhythm for my words, but this is all that I can find around the small bits of breath my lungs are giving me.

"Looks just like you," she says.

We both turn our heads again to watch Elsie move, the way she steps sideways on the balls of her feet as she practice swings with one racquet, then swaps it out for another.

"She play like you?" Mary asks.

"She does," I say, and my heart does this big swell thing that it does when I talk about Elsie and know that what I'm saying is true and right.

Mary nods, turns her hand upward to touch the side of her mouth. The word in black ink on her wrist is *truth*, all lowercase, in a script of letters that touch each other at the curves. "She'll do fine, then."

I stand in the middle of the tennis store, between the two loves of my life, watching my child move the way I used to, and I wish I believed that was true.

Fifteen

Mary had a ponytail then. Long and blonde, with high-sprayed bangs that tried to claw at her forehead. She didn't have any curves. None of us tennis girls did. Just long and lanky, with reaches that seemed impossible for our height.

"What do you say, Maggie-May?" she'd say, and swat me on the ass with a racquet as she slid to her place on the court behind me, her pockets bulging with tennis balls. It was part of our ritual, the way we started every match.

"I say..." And I'd flip her the bird in response. Such a dirty thing back then, that simple upturn of a finger. I look at it now and laugh to myself. What rebels we thought we were. Such big shots.

We were *the* girls' doubles team for Petersonville High. Her, long ponytail swinging from side to side as she moved, blue eyes watching everything that happened on the court, her thin calves bouncing as she rolled on her toes. And then me, not as tall, nowhere near as pale. I had the beginnings of curves where she didn't, but nothing to speak of, and thick, muscular calves. I was growing my dark bob out and it plagued me constantly—the bangs always pinned back by a million barrettes, the back never staying in its short, tight tail.

"Bird is the word," she'd say, and raise her one eyebrow into an arching *V*. And we'd be ready, just like that.

She had this serve, this high, slow lob that was just impossible to hit. A lob like that, it's called the Hail Mary in tennis circles. I think opponents first thought it would never make it over the net, or they thought its slow height would make it an easy return. Then it landed, aced, and they were determined to hit the next one. Which they'd miss, and then they'd be psyching themselves out for the next two or three.

It got so that we'd actually get a crowd—unheard of for something as non-cool as tennis—and they'd be chanting, "Hail Mary, Hail Mary," every time she served.

I couldn't serve like that to save my life, but I could dig and return just about anything on my good days. It wasn't something I had to think about. I could just do, my body always reacting faster than my brain could understand.

We played hard and good, an unbreakable team from our

freshman year to our senior year. And that last year, we went all the way to the top, or what was the top in those days—state finals. And we swept them, nothing to it. Our opponents barely got a chance to unpack their racquets and start swinging before she and I had taken over the court, teamed up, doing what we did best.

"What do you say, Maggie-May?" Mary asked, after we'd won. We were spending the night in Trumansburg after the finals, draped over each other on the hotel bed, pretending to do calculus, but really just reliving our kills, our aces, the way we'd tromped the Waverly girls into the dirt.

"I say..." And I flipped her the bird, like I always did. Mary nipped it with the point of her teeth, laughing against my skin.

"Bird *is* the word," she said.

And we were together, just like that. I'd never kissed a girl before, had never kissed anyone but one boy, a tennis player too, and that had been meat and onion and something I never wanted to go back to. Mary's mouth against mine was soft and sweet, wet as misty rain. Her breath tasted like sweet ice tea and the mint gum she chewed while she played. I thought maybe all girls tasted like this, or maybe it was just Mary, sugar and spice.

I wasn't sure how to touch her with anything but my mouth, just tongue and teeth and lips. My body wanted to move, to press and arch, but I didn't know how.

"Like this, Maggie-May," she said, and I wondered how she knew so much, how she knew to put her fingers between my thighs with that soft, fluttered touch. She took my hand, covered it and slid it over the length of her waist, up beneath her T-shirt, then down. On my own, I touched her barely there hips, the lean muscles of her thigh.

I came for her, that first time, my first time, and I hadn't even gotten undressed.

Deuce

Being the best at high school tennis didn't amount to much when it came to paying for college. You either had money and went to Cornell, or you had nothing and you went to the local community college.

Tennis didn't buy us an entry into the big C, so Mary and I roomed our way through a two-year degree in doing everything but going to class.

If it was nice out, we were outside, hitting balls on the court, practicing. When we weren't at official practice or at games, we'd play whoever would put their quarters up. It wasn't nice, the way we whipped them so badly, and it sure wasn't a challenge, but Mary and I needed to play the same way we needed to breathe, the same way we needed to fuck.

If it was raining or too damn hot, we were inside, opening each other's bodies, tongues and fingers and thighs, splaying each other open with the same fierceness that we had on the court. In two years, Mary's body hadn't changed that much— lean as a boy, small pale breasts that fit perfectly into my palms and butted their nipples against my thumbs—but my own had curved, widening into something as creamy and soft-churned as butter. Boys gave me that look, something that I both feared and craved, but it was Mary I gave my body to, my mind to.

"Come for me, Maggie-May," she'd say a hundred times a day. On the court. Off the court. Passing me in the halls. And it was enough to make me wet all the way to the inside of my knees. She'd crook her fingers at me from across the room, that little come-hither that I loved inside me, and I'd feel myself open up for her, wet and wanting.

A month before graduation, we were lazing in our dorm— we'd pushed the two single beds together to make something that fit us both, always laughing about how Mary was so skinny she kept falling into the crack in the middle.

"Almost out of here," Mary said. We'd never talked about what came next. Just kept our heads down and our racquets up and our bodies together in the quiet dark of our room.

If you squinted just right, the freckles on Mary's back made the shape of a tennis racquet. I grabbed my pink highlighter off the floor, connected the dots with the neon marker and drew in the oval curves and the straight string lines while she talked.

Mary turned mid-draw, making one of my lines go all squiggly. "What are you going to do after?"

I shrugged, re-capped the marker. It hurt me, somehow, that she'd asked *you* and not *we*, but I didn't know why. We hadn't talked about the future, but somehow I'd assumed we had one. "I don't know. I've got that summer camp offer in Connecticut. But I'd rather hang out and watch you play tennis."

I dipped my face into the curve of her neck, met her skin with a soft parting of my lips and teeth. She tasted like sunshine, like sweet and sour, like lemonade. I thought I could live off of nothing more than that.

"You should take it," she said. "I'm not going to play tennis anymore."

I'd laughed. Her saying no tennis was like her say no more fucking. But she looked serious. "What?" I asked. "You think I should take it?"

"Yes," she said.

My stomach was doing odd things, rolling over and over, too tight. "Why?"

She took the marker from me without answering. "My turn," she said. But she didn't use the marker. She used her tongue, slid it over my skin, drawing with the heat of her mouth. Nipple to nipple, the mole on the side of my shoulder, the birthmark near my belly button, the soft point of skin between my thighs.

I wanted to ask whether she meant the tennis thing or not, but she was dragging her tongue along the wet heat of my center, dipping her fingers in. She played my body the same way she played tennis. Instinct and passion, competition and drive, forcing me over the edge even as I begged her to wait, to let me play too.

I took the Connecticut job, taught summer camp for two months. I wrote Mary every week, letters full of longing and lust, stories about the summer camp kids, about their tennis skills or lack thereof. I wanted to make her laugh, to make her wish she was with me, to keep us as close as we'd always been.

That whole time, Mary wrote me once. Just once. Her letter was a page long and it said nothing much at all. Still, I held on to it as a sign, as gospel that she still loved me, still wanted me, still ached for me.

I couldn't wait to go home.

Thirty

By the time I got there, Mary was already gone. She'd taken a job with some smoke-jumping fire crew out in Oregon. I hid my heartbreak by breaking my back on the tennis court and by courting women who looked nothing like her. Fucking my way through the country club where I worked—married women who hadn't been touched in years, mothers and wives with diamonds as big as my fist. Not a one of them could play tennis or play me, but I didn't care. I just needed a place to put my fingers, my fist, the sharp point of my despair.

There were two things Mary never did tell me, things I didn't find out until much later. The first was that back when we were in high school, Cornell had offered her a spot—a free ride on their tennis team. She'd turned them down, said she didn't want to go without me.

The other thing she never told me? That she'd loved me. More than anything. Even more than tennis.

Forty

"Do you still play?" Mary is popping a tennis ball from one hand to the other, the counter between us like a net that can't be crossed. In the corner, Elsie has found a racquet she likes. The sound of her swinging it, over and over, cutting the air, whistles beneath our words.

"Nah," I say. "You?"

"Yeah," she says. "I missed it too much. There's an indoor court for us old people, over in Hillsboro. You should come sometime."

"Maybe I will."

"This one, mom," Elsie says. She's picked a good racquet, and an expensive one, of course. But it's easy to tell it feels good in her hand, the way she carries it, holds it, the pink flush in her cheeks as she looks at it. I remember how that felt, to own everything and nothing, to not be able to see beyond what was in my hand and my heart.

"You're sure?" I ask.

"Yep."

"Well, let's get it."

Mary is silent, watching.

For the first time, my daughter notices her. How selfish we all are as teenagers, I think. Not in a bad way, but in a real and true way. Everything is glorious. Everything is ours.

"Hi," Elsie says. Sudden and shy.

Mary smiles her lopsided smile and takes the racquet from my daughter, the one who looks so like me. For a moment, their hands touch, and two small globes come together, crisscross, lob into each other, soft and high. "You play like your mom," Mary says. "I can tell."

"My mom played tennis?"

Our eyes meet over Elsie's head. Why haven't I told her? I don't have an answer for that. Maybe because if I'd started, I wasn't sure where I would have stopped, how much of the story I would have told.

"Jeez, mom, you played tennis?" Elsie is looking at her racquet with a look I've never seen before. Whether it's pride or disgust, I have no idea.

"Yeah," I say. I slide my credit card across the counter and Mary takes it. Our hands stop at the middle line of the space between us, don't cross or touch. "I wasn't very good though. Mary here was, though. She was the best."

"She was?"

"Yep," I say, and my heart does that big swell again. "The very best."

Game Point

Mary's body is everything I remember plus all that it's become. Hard and soft, long and lean. Her stomach curves out a little, her breasts rest farther down. When I take her hand and press it between my thighs, her skin is rough with time. It makes me want to cry and to cry out, the sweet feel of her fingers, the painful press of what's been lost and found.

My own fingers inside her are wrapped in heat and wet, in the tight press of her body. She kisses me, hard, tongue and teeth. Together we are both careful and ravenous, aware of our hunger, barely willing to be aware of our frailty.

She makes me come the way I haven't come in a long time. That kind that rushes out of you like breath and leaves you empty and falling. The kind that makes it impossible to tell the difference between losing and love.

"You left me," I say, and I'm sobbing. Stupid. Tears.

"You left me first," she says. Her fingers are still inside me, filling me.

"You"—I am hiccupping like a child, like a teenage girl in love—"told me to."

"I loved you," she says, as though this explains anything at all.

Love. Again.

A few miles from here there is an indoor tennis court where a tall, thin, strong woman named Mary will hit a high, soft serve that could have been named for her, she sends it sailing so perfectly. On the other side of the long white net, someone else will wait, racquet in hand, poised to receive this thing, this deceptively easy and oh-so-hard thing that Mary has offered.

That someone will not be me. I will be at my daughter's high school, watching Elsie dig in, swing hard and sweet and pure, watching her return everything that comes at her without fear, wondering where she learned it.

And then I will remember Mary's mouth against mine before she left this morning, the press of her tongue, the lemonade taste of her lips. The way she whispers, *"Zero, Love,"* as if they are not the same thing. And I will rejoice to be on the receiving end of that high, sweet swing of faith.

GODDESS IN
A RED-AND-
BLUE SPEEDO

D. L. King

All right, this is going to sound like a lie, but it isn't. I actually won a trip to Hawaii once. I sent in a postcard to a radio contest and two weeks later I found out I was the winner of the grand prize—yup, you guessed it—a trip to Hawaii. I got laid off two weeks after that—'cause nothing's for free—but within a month I was off to the islands.

I did one of those resort scuba dives and after that, I was hooked. As soon as I got home, got another job and could afford it, I signed up for a National Association of Underwater Instructors (NAUI) certification course. And after hours in a classroom, learning mathematical formulas and safety and history, our instructor, George, announced we were finally going to get wet—in a swimming pool but, hey, it was water.

There were seven of us: a straight couple who were getting married in the spring and planning a honeymoon to the Bahamas; a gay couple who had also done a resort dive while on vacation and gotten hooked; and two girls who were best friends who dared each other to sign up. I was currently unattached, so I was the odd woman out. By the time the pool sessions got started, we were all psyched.

We met each other at the college pool that shared space with the scuba school. The guys headed off to their locker room and the four of us girls headed off to ours. The soon-to-be-married Cheryl changed into a purple, iridescent bikini. The rest of us changed into our Jantzens and Speedos. At least it was nice to see that, as New Yorkers in March, we were all fish-belly white. After all, it really doesn't matter what you look like in a bathing suit because no one's ever happy. So we filed self-consciously out of the locker room and into the pool area with our towels and brand new masks, fins and weight belts.

George was waiting for us by the pool. "You won't need your gear tonight. We're just going to have swimming trials." Everyone dropped their stuff against the wall and wandered back to the edge. "This is Lorna. She's another instructor and a dive master. She's going to be working with you in the pool sessions."

She had short sun-bleached blonde hair, long muscular legs, a completely flat stomach and a deep tan. Lorna was a goddess in a red-and-blue Speedo with a racer back. As if I hadn't felt self-conscious enough.

The echo of her whistle got everyone's attention. "All right people; you're going to swim four laps and then tread water and/or float for fifteen minutes. I'm not trying to scare you, but you'll have to be able to pass this water competency test before you can complete the rest of the course and do your open water dives. Now, everyone in the pool."

The smell of the chlorine was pretty strong. I figured my eyes were going to be really red by the time we were finished but I wasn't worried about passing the test; I knew I was a strong swimmer. George told us we could use any strokes we wanted to swim the laps and that it wasn't a race; we just needed to be able to do it any way we could. Another bleat of Lorna's whistle and we were off. Larry, Cheryl's fiancé, and Carson and I were at the lead. We finished our laps several minutes before the fourth fastest swimmer and began our water treading.

I could tread water for a pretty long time, but I was tired. I looked up and saw Lorna watching me. "Do I have to tread for a certain amount of time or can I float?"

"Nope," she said. "You can float the whole fifteen minutes, if you want. The object is to keep from drowning for a while, if you have to."

Pretty sure she'd save me, I thought about drowning, but then I remembered what the world looked like under the ocean. "Thanks," I said and immediately stopped treading water and leaned back, let my feet come up to the surface, put my arms behind my head and relaxed. My ears were in the water, but I'm sure I heard her laugh.

Everyone managed to complete the test. Cheryl was the last one. She was exhausted but George assured her she could still finish and get certified. Carson's partner, Blaine, had a hell of a time with the treading/floating exercise. The guy had absolutely no body fat and kept sinking. He had a great body, but I felt sorry for him. I always knew my tits and love of ice cream would pay off.

Over the next few weeks we all met at the pool and learned various things about breathing underwater. I never got tired of watching Lorna either giving direction from the pool deck or, better yet, swimming underwater with us. I tried really hard not to look at the way the red of her bathing suit squeezed her flat stomach and smoothed down between her legs, encasing the slightly raised pillow of her sex, or the way the blue around her arms accentuated her small breasts. My excitement mounted through the week, until Thursday would roll around and I could see my goddess again. I took great pains to make sure she never actually caught me staring at her.

The week after, we learned cheerful things, like clearing a facemask that had filled with water and buddy breathing (with George) when you ran out of air, and finally, learning to make an emergency ascent with no air at all. We were finally done with the pool part of the course. Walking back into the classroom the following week to take the final written test, I felt a real sense of accomplishment—and a bit of a letdown, when I noticed my blonde-haired goddess wasn't there. The test wasn't easy, but I'd studied hard and I passed with flying colors.

I signed up for the open water test, which would be a beach dive and a couple of boat dives. No Lorna there, either. I really wished I'd had the nerve to talk to her and maybe get her number, but now it was too late.

Shortly after I received my NAUI Worldwide SCUBA Diver card in the mail, I got a call from George. He said the shop was organizing a trip to Mexico and asked me if I'd like to go.

I got the details and requested the vacation time. This would be my first dive somewhere beautiful. My open water checkout dives were all in the cold, gray water off the coast of New York where you were lucky if you had three feet of visibility and didn't freeze to death, even in the summer. I could swear my last dive in the cold Atlantic only afforded about six inches of visibility.

Finally the time came. I couldn't get out of a meeting and so wasn't able to fly down with everyone. I had to take a later flight. When I finally arrived, I checked in to the hotel and left a message for George letting him know I was there. The next morning, he called at six a.m. and told me to meet everyone downstairs for breakfast. Our first dive was at eight o'clock. When I got down to the restaurant, the first person I saw was Lorna.

"Hey, I'm so glad you're here," she said. "I thought, maybe, you were going to miss the trip when you weren't on the plane."

My mouth was open, but I couldn't seem to make it work right. Finally, I managed to get the word, *meeting*, out. She gave me a quizzical look and a little frown before saying she was glad I made it.

God, what a loser!

There were seven of us, plus George and Lorna, on the boat. The only people from my class were Carson and Blaine and again, I was the only single. George told me he'd be my dive buddy. I was a little disappointed that Lorna wasn't going to be my buddy, but I figured, after the way I acted in the restaurant, why would she want to? Once in the water, I forgot all about wishing Lorna was my dive buddy. The beauty of the under-water world was all encompassing. I didn't want to come back up when George gave me the signal. I still had almost half a tank of air.

Back on the boat, everyone was exhilarated, talking about all the things we'd seen. George explained that different body types use different amounts of air and when the first person began to get low, we'd all surface. We had lunch on the boat and traveled to the next site, diving about an hour after we'd surfaced from the first dive. I went on two more dives the next day but opted out on the third day to go to the beach and sightsee.

Tired from the sun, I got back to my room to take a nap and was awakened by the phone. It was Lorna, telling me they'd booked a night dive and asking me if I'd like to go. She said it was really special and even more beautiful than daytime dives. I couldn't say no and made plans to meet at the boat dock in a few hours.

There were only three other divers. Blaine had come alone

and so George paired us up as buddies. We were given chemical light sticks to attach to our equipment and handheld dive lights to use underwater.

It wasn't a very deep dive, only about thirty feet at the deepest, but it was really amazing to see all the neon colors of the nocturnal sea creatures. About halfway into the dive, I took a breath and got a mouth full of water. I took the regulator out of my mouth and saw that the hose had broken. Not panicking, I went for my spare regulator, but couldn't find it. I grabbed Blaine and made the signal for "out of air" and the signal for "buddy breathing" so that we could both share his air. He panicked and dislodged my mask while shoving his regulator at my face. I didn't get enough time to both breathe and clear my mask before he took it back. I waited for the regulator to be given back to me, but it didn't come. I banged on my tank with my knife to get the dive master's attention but I was blind and really out of air by that time.

I began an emergency assent to the surface but felt someone grab my ankle to try to bring me back down. I kicked them and continued upward. Panicked, out of air, I came very close to drowning, but I finally broke the surface and gasped in the air. Lorna surfaced right behind me, and Blaine right behind her. Bobbing on the surface, she signaled the boat, which made it to our location just as everyone else surfaced.

Lorna didn't leave my side. She got me a towel and a bottle of water and put her arm around me. I kept apologizing for ruining everyone's dive and she kept assuring me that everything was all right. Once at the dock, she took care of my equipment and helped me off the boat. "C'mon," she said, "I'm taking you to your room. Where's your key?"

"In my shorts in my bag," I replied, "but you don't have to. Really. I'm okay."

"What's your room number?" I told her and carrying my equipment, she herded me into the elevator. She followed me off the elevator and down the hall, opened my door and herded me inside. "Go take a shower. I'm going to order some food. What do you want?"

"I don't know," I said. "I'm not hungry, really. Get whatever you want." Beginning to feel better, I grabbed a pair of shorts and a T-shirt and stepped into the bathroom. When I came out, dressed and drying my hair, Lorna was waiting for me.

"Do you have an extra pair of shorts and a T-shirt I could borrow? I don't want to leave you and I could really use a shower, too."

I handed her some clothes and heard the shower running shortly after. All I could think about was how it would have been really nice to share the shower with her, but I knew she wasn't thinking about that; she was just thinking about my safety. The food arrived and the waiter wheeled the cart into the room. I heard the water shut off and soon Lorna was standing beside the cart, wearing my new DIVE MEXICO shirt and a pair of gym shorts.

"I didn't know whether you were a vegetarian or not, so I didn't order meat. I hope that's all right."

She'd ordered guacamole and a couple of orders of cheese enchiladas with beans and rice. "I'm not a vegetarian, but you just happened to hit all my favorite Mexican foods," I said.

She laughed. "Mine, too. Cool. Want some water or soda? I can go to the machine." She came back with a couple bottles of water and we sat down to decimate the food. I hadn't realized how hungry I really was.

"Yeah, diving'll do that to you," she said.

"Almost drowning will, too," I replied.

She put her hand on my thigh. "I was so worried about you."

Without raising my head, I raised my eyes. "Well, I guess it would be pretty bad if one of your divers drowned on your watch. I'm really sorry."

"Yeah, it would be, but I wasn't thinking about that. I was worried about *you*." She slid her hand a little farther up my leg. "I, uh…I really like you and…I was worried and… Well, I don't know how you feel about that, but…"

I looked her in the eyes and leaned toward her, causing her hand to slide up to my crotch. She tried to move it, but I covered it with mine and slid it back. "I like you too," I said and gave her a peck on the lips. I started to draw back, but she caught the back of my neck and pressed my mouth to hers, this time taking the lead, kissing me hard. I ran my fingers through her still-wet hair and when we finally broke apart, I studied her face.

"I didn't think… I didn't know whether…"

"I caught you staring at me during class a few times," she said. "Every time I tried to talk to you, you'd run off. It was like you were Speedy Gonzalez or something. I never saw anyone take a shower, change and get out of the locker room faster than you." She kissed me again. "Just a minute," she said, and wheeled the room service cart into the hallway. "Just in case they come back looking for this."

I was waiting for her in the middle of the room. She closed and locked the door and put her arms around me, kissing me with more urgency as she walked me backward until the backs of my legs bumped the bed. Pushing me onto the bed, she followed, her lips still on mine and her knees on either side of my hips. Coming up for air, she looked at me and said, "You are so hot," as she slid her hands under my T-shirt, sliding it up my body.

I hadn't put a bra on after my shower and her smile widened as she exposed my breasts. "Damn, woman. Fuck, you're gorgeous." Her mouth latched onto a breast and her hand stroked the other one. She lowered her torso down and just before our crotches met, she pushed her other hand down my shorts, holding it prisoner with her body as she stroked me.

She switched from my breast to my mouth, kissing me quickly before taking her hand out of my shorts, pulling my T-shirt over my head and throwing it on the floor. "You okay wi—" she started to ask before I grabbed her head and pulled her down for another kiss.

As I kissed her, her hands flew back to my shorts. She undid the button and drew the zipper down and I raised my hips while she pulled the shorts and my underwear off in one motion.

"Wow, look at you with the Brazilian, girlfriend," she exclaimed. "Nice." She slid down my torso until she was face to pussy with me and pressed her fingers against my bare mound. "So smooth." She licked both sides before following with a lick up the center.

"Bathing suits, you know," I said. "Why so surprised. What about you?" I asked.

"That's for me to know and you to find out later," she said, going back to licking and sucking on my pussy lips. "So soft and smooth and perfect," she said, speaking to my cunt. "I, I didn't know... I thought you weren't into me and I was reading the signals wrong. I caught you staring at me a bunch of times during the class and I thought you might be...but then you never said anything or even tried to talk to me at all. When I'd come out of the locker room you'd already be gone." She buried her hands under my ass and lifted me up for a better angle. She spread my lips wide with her fingers.

"A bunch of times?" I asked. I couldn't believe she'd caught me. I had tried to be so careful.

"Uh-huh," she said, nodding her head up and down between

my legs. "I thought you were either interested in me or there was something odd about the way I looked—and I was pretty sure there wasn't anything odd about the way I looked."

I'd been playing with her hair, but now I smacked the side of her head, lightly. "Yes, we both know you're gorgeous."

"Hey!" She circled my clit with a finger and the feeling took the last smart thing I was going to say completely out of my head and replaced it with a moan.

"Yeah, baby, that's right." She inserted first one finger and then a second, languorously fucking me. She used her other hand to lightly stroke my clit. "And, besides, you're the one who's gorgeous. Jesus, woman, look at you." Her eyes looked up from between my legs to my face and I met her gaze as a first, gentle spasm rolled through me. I griped her with my thighs, imprisoning her face in my line of vision. My eyes never left hers as she stroked me to completion.

My legs relaxed and she was freed to climb up my body and lie next to me on the bed. We lay together for a few minutes, while I caught my breath before I turned to look at her. "You're still dressed," I said.

"Well, I guess I didn't have time..."

"I'm hungry. Are you hungry?"

"I guess so," she said. "I mean, we just ate but I guess I could have something."

"Nachos."

"Um, yeah, we could have some nachos..."

"And maybe a drink. Or maybe I should ravish you now." Completely energized, I reached for her shirt.

"I vote for ravishment. We really shouldn't drink if we're diving tomorrow."

"Oh," I said, frowning, "I wasn't planning on diving tomorrow."

"But it's the last diving day of the trip." She studied me with serious eyes. "You have to dive tomorrow. If you don't, you might never dive again. You can't let something like this throw you. You have to get right back out there. It was a fluke. Your skills are strong. You're a good diver."

"Really?" I asked. "You really think that? But I wasn't paying attention. I didn't notice where the captain stowed my spare regulator. I was stupid."

"Yes, I really think you're a good diver. You're not stupid. It was an accident. I saw you. You were looking for your regulator exactly where you'd been taught. You have to dive tomorrow. And now I'm ready for nachos and ice tea. You can ravish me after. But you should probably put some clothes on before we go downstairs—I'm just saying."

I dove the next morning. Just a one-tank dive because I was tired. But I dove, partnered with the goddess with the short blonde hair and red-and-blue Speedo. Back at the hotel, it was my turn to do the ravishing.

That was ten years ago. Yes, I'm still diving. And to think it all started with a random free trip to Hawaii.

CYMONE'S DOMINATRIX

Paisley Smith

Appolonia sat at the table with the Hellene women, watching the other *gladiatrices* in their revelry. She sipped her wine. The games began tomorrow and she wanted to be at her best, not nursing woes from too much drink. The *editor* of the games had gone to great expense to treat the fighters to a lavish feast. Although the tribeswomen from the North—the Dacians and Caledonians—drank to excess, most of the Greek women, including Appolonia, only consumed watered wine.

Heady fragrances of roasted meat fused with the distinctive musk belonging to the forty female warriors. Laughter and bodacious bragging punctuated the balmy night air.

A fight amongst two Pictish women broke out across the room, but rather than join in, the other women moved aside and allowed the two to pummel each other until one of the trainers came in and separated the brawlers.

Appolonia sighed. Such nights always passed thus. Extreme drinking and overeating among the women tended to be the norm. But on the sands, the barbarian women relied on their girth rather than their skill. Such celebrating only made them fiercer opponents. The Hellenes employed technique and savvy to defeat their adversaries.

Still, the carousing reached an unusual height tonight. Doubtless, Appolonia thought, due to the knowledge that many of the *gladiatrices* in Marcus Flavius's *ludus* would be forced to fight against each other tomorrow.

Each particular ethnic group tended to keep quarters with their own kind, but as members of the same house, the women all felt a familial kinship despite their origin of birth.

Appolonia finished her wine and looked across the table to where Cymone, another Hellene, sat staring into her cup.

Cymone. *Gladiatrix prima.* She dominated on the sands, knowing just how long to drag out a fight so that the crowd cheered her to victory again and again, knowing how to make a spectacle of dealing the death blow to anyone unlucky enough to have to face her. She was a true champion, an entertainer who'd risen far above her status as a slave to become one of the most celebrated *gladiatrices* of her time. A scar marred her olive-skinned cheek, but to Appolonia, the imperfection only made Cymone that much more intriguing, that much more beautiful.

For all her prowess in the arena, however, Cymone delighted in darker pleasures of the flesh and Appolonia was pleased the *gladiatrix* had chosen her as a lover. Most nights, they lay in each other's arms, bringing each other release before succumbing to the god Hypnos's spell. But on the evening before an appearance on the sands, Cymone allowed Appolonia a far firmer hand.

Appolonia squeezed her thighs together in anticipation. Any moment, Cymone would rise, giving the signal that they were to continue the festivities in a more intimate setting.

Cymone had explained her taboo yearning, but only once. Through submission, she found strength to face her most dreaded foes. Through pain and surrender, she discovered the fortitude to persevere despite any odds.

Appolonia admired Cymone *and* she loved her. In dominating her, Appolonia found her own strength.

Cymone lifted her head and with a shrug swept her long black hair over her shoulder, revealing the voluptuous curves beneath her tunic. Appolonia's stomach knotted when their gazes connected. Her mouth watered at the knowledge she would soon be tormenting the pebbled nipples beneath the thin fabric of Cymone's garment.

"Have you partaken of the merriment long enough?" Cymone asked, her voice deep and husky. The flash in her dark green eyes teemed with illicit promises.

"Yes," Appolonia whispered. The word came out strangled. She sounded too eager, too easy. But that's what she was where Cymone was concerned.

In that one instant, the *gladiatrix prima* became Appolonia's property; lower than any slave and hers to command.

Appolonia swallowed. She steeled herself for what was to come. "To your cell. Remove your tunic and await me on your hands and knees."

At once, Cymone shot to her feet. As soon as her lover had left the dining hall, Appolonia closed her eyes and tried to still her hammering heart. Wetness gathered between her legs, dampening her own tunic. The thought of Cymone stripping herself bare and awaiting punishment in the most humiliating of positions caused Appolonia's blood to heat and thrum like thunder through her veins. That the proud warrior would willingly defer to her made Appolonia's chest swell with pride.

But for now, she would make Cymone wait. A smile tugged at Appolonia's lips as she poured another goblet of watered wine and began to sip.

With trembling hands, Cymone carefully removed her tunic, folded it and placed it across the chair in the corner of her cell. She glanced at the barred window on the door. The guards moving about in the hallway would surely wonder why she had climbed onto the cot on her hands and knees—but she had orders to follow.

A tingle swept over her naked skin as she planted her palms on the cot. She debated pressing her knees together, but that would most certainly displease Appolonia. Instead, Cymone set her knees on either edge of the cot. Her eyes drifted shut as she imagined the intense pleasure and pain that would be dealt to her soon. All thoughts of the arena tomorrow faded and there was only this moment. Her pulse pounded in her throat. Her channel clenched and her rim burned in anticipation of the upcoming invasion. Fingers. Tongue. Other objects...

She inhaled deeply, feeling the breath spread to every portion of her body. Her own juices slickened her folds, preparing her.

Time passed. Her hands ached. Her knees burned. Blood pounded in her temples, but she would not move. She would not displease her lover.

Finally, the door swung open, grating on its hinges. Cymone did not lift her head to gaze upon the black-haired beauty, but her stomach tensed with a wild mixture of joy and expectation. Her arms shook from sheer sexual hunger. She squeezed her eyes shut and capable hands slid smoothly down her spine and over her bottom. Her clitoris pulsed as she awaited her lover's touch. She gulped. *Please...*

One fingertip edged closer, so close... If only she shifted

slightly, the finger would brush her aching flesh. Cymone did shift.

She was rewarded with a smart slap to one asscheek. Her teeth sank into her bottom lip as fire licked through her skin, settling into a sensuous, warm throb. Her blood thickened as it coursed through swollen veins. It seemed as if her consciousness spiraled deep within, leaving only her senses—to feel, to experience, to glory in all her lover intended to mete out to her.

Cymone's breathing deepened as a soft palm kneaded the place that had just been punished.

"You will receive pleasure when I decide," Appolonia bit out.

Cymone couldn't stifle the whimper that welled in her throat. Her body ached to be touched.

Another smack reignited the fire in her backside. "Off the cot. No. You may not stand. On your hands and knees, slave."

Cymone trembled as she clambered down from the cot onto the cool stone floor. Appolonia slipped off her tunic and Cymone gazed upon the taut, muscular form. High, small breasts perched above a rippled abdomen. And lower, sinewy lines delineated the V of Appolonia's denuded crotch. A blushing clitoris peeped between two dusky folds.

Cymone's mouth watered as she imagined teasing that succulent flesh with her tongue.

Appolonia parted her legs and motioned Cymone closer. At once, Cymone crawled to her lover and burrowed her tongue between the sweet nether lips. She couldn't get enough. Her lover's fragrance and taste filled her senses. Juices dribbled onto her tongue as she lapped and explored, never able to get close enough, to delve deeply enough.

Fingers threaded into her hair, tugging hard enough to set her scalp on fire and then alternately pulling her mouth impossibly closer. Cymone reached for her lover's thighs and at once a tight yank on her hair drew her head back. Breathless, she lifted her gaze to Appolonia's.

Her black eyes were flinty in the dim light. "I did not give you permission to touch." She tugged Cymone's hair again for emphasis. "Hands behind your back."

Cymone laced her fingers behind her as she was drawn once more to the glistening prize between her lover's legs. As Cymone explored with her tongue, Appolonia rocked, grinding the lust-damp flesh against Cymone's mouth until she felt her lips bruising from the force. Velvet skin with hard bone underneath undulated with quickening ferocity. Cymone could scarcely breathe when Appolonia spread wider and dipped to ride her mouth and tongue.

Oh, to die here instead of bleeding and broken on the sands...

Cymone kissed and licked and sucked until Appolonia shuddered and her breathing became ragged. Sweet nectar gushed onto Cymone's tongue and she knew she'd brought her lover to orgasm. Her pulse accelerated. The most exquisite torture awaited now that she'd dulled the edge of Appolonia's need.

Appolonia's fingers caressed Cymone's head and she gloried in what she knew would be short-lived praise.

"On your feet," Appolonia ordered, her voice cracking as she spoke.

Triumph flitted through Cymone's breast as she stood. Her knees shook.

"Bend over. Put your hands down on the cot."

Veins thrumming with hot bursts of blood, Cymone obeyed.

A foot pressed against her ankle. "Spread your legs."

Cymone gulped and parted her feet.

"Wider."

If she resisted, pleasing punishment awaited. If she complied...

Oh, if she did as she was bidden, unspeakable tortures of the flesh would be dealt her. Bracing herself, Cymone walked her feet even farther apart.

"You're wet," Appolonia murmured.

Everything inside Cymone tightened to the snapping point. Her breathing grew shallow as she listened to the sound of Appolonia removing a leather strap from their bag of *delights*.

The tip of the leather teased up the inside of one thigh, stopping to lick lightly at the pulsing flesh between before slithering down the other thigh. Three hard successive smacks fell on her cheeks and rather than twist away from the pain, she pushed toward it, wanting it, wanting to be swept toward the very edge of endurance.

Cymone quivered as fingers teased along her drenched slit. *Please...*

But rather than plunge inside, the fingers trailed around her hip and reached underneath to drift over the sensitive skin of her belly before moving upward. Cymone held her breath as those same digits toyed with her nipple. Her shoulders shook as she struggled to keep her palms planted firmly on the cot. A cry escaped her lips when Appolonia pinched and gave her nipple the most exquisite tug. Sensation shot from Cymone's breast straight to her throbbing clitoris.

More blows striped her bottom until she heard her own moans reverberating off the stone walls of the cell. She was poised for release, but her tormentor had other plans.

Two fingers slid up inside Cymone's tight channel. At once, she felt herself beginning to spasm, but just as bliss hovered near, the invasion ended and the fingertips nudged her nether hole.

Her mind screamed *No*, but her body betrayed her. Dipping her back, she offered herself to be prodded like a slave eunuch. One slippery finger eased past her rim and burrowed inside.

Although she'd only drunk a small amount of watered wine, she felt intoxicated. Her head hung as she reveled in the slow, sensual invasion. Her muscles relaxed as she opened to the lazy thrusts of the finger inside her tight ass. When Appolonia's finger slid all the way inside, her other fingers flirted with the needy flesh of her sex. Cymone tried, but in vain, to arch and bend to receive more contact. Frustration welled. It was no use. Her lover was too experienced to give in to her whims just yet.

When the finger withdrew, Cymone let out a moan of disappointment.

The strap fell on the cot and Appolonia pointed to the bag. "Fetch the *olisbos*."

With lush warmth still radiating through her backside, she moved toward the bag to retrieve the thick leather phallus her lover used on her in the most torturous ways. Doubtless, it would find its way into her recently violated bottom. Cymone tried to swallow, but couldn't. Anticipation fired through her veins.

"On your knees!" Appolonia ordered.

Cymone dropped to the floor and crawled the rest of the way to where the bag lay crumpled in the corner. The stones hurt her knees and palms, but she welcomed the discomfort. Her reward for obedience would come later. She pawed open the bag and retrieved the scarlet leather-covered *olisbos*.

"The salve, too."

Oh, yes. Her bottom indeed. Cymone wet her dry lips with the tip of her tongue as she removed the jar of salve from the bag.

Appolonia sat on the cot and motioned for Cymone to assume the position over her knees. Dutifully, Cymone passed the *olisbos* and the salve to Appolonia before she bent across her lover's lap. She knew well that the *olisbos* would not be used gently on her. Heart pounding, she waited as Appolonia took her time tò coat the wicked sex toy with a generous amount of the greasy salve.

"Spread your cheeks."

Cymone swallowed thickly as she reached behind to draw her asscheeks apart.

"Tell me where you want this."

Cymone's breathing hitched. "In my...in my ass, Dominatrix."

A hard swat landed on her bottom before the thick tip of the *olisbos* nudged against her nether hole and pushed inside. Cymone gritted her teeth as the smooth, greased leather slid fully into her resistant flesh. Fire spread around her rim as she stretched to receive the intrusion.

As soon as she adjusted to the feel of the device inside her, it retreated only to plunge into her again. Her nails dug into the muscled flesh of her backside as she withstood thrust after hard thrust. Appolonia wrapped her free hand around Cymone's throat, anchoring her, dominating her.

The noise of wet suction, of punctuated breaths and of Cymone's impassioned groans filled the cell. Pain twisted into pleasure. Her legs trembled. Her grip on her own bottom slipped and she struggled to hold firm, to keep herself open to anything her dominatrix wanted to mete out to her.

Release hovered close. The hand around Cymone's neck tightened dangerously, reminding her just who was in control of her pleasure. That knowledge shattered her. Hard bliss crashed over her like a tempest over the sea, a savage storm of sensation that radiated outward from the spot where the massive *olisbos* filled her to utter capacity. She cried out, unable to quell the long, low moans that escaped her throat. The pleasure seemed unending as Appolonia continued to urge the instrument in and out of her. Cymone wilted over her mistress's lap, whimpering and shuddering as the waves finally eddied and tailed off.

The *olisbos* slipped out and soothing hands pampered her, rubbing her bottom and smoothing over her back and hair. Cymone gathered herself and moved in tandem with her lover onto the cot where Appolonia held her and kissed her for what seemed like hours.

Tears welled and spilled down Cymone's cheeks at the stark contrast of pain followed by *this*. She loved Appolonia. She'd loved her since the *lanista*, Flavius, had bought her and brought her to the *ludus* three years prior. But with their future so uncertain, she'd never given voice to the words. What good would it bring to love another only to die on the sands? The life of a *gladiatrix* was a hard one.

Appolonia cradled her head and sought her lips, which Cymone readily gave. As their tongues twisted, sparred and explored, Cymone's hands roamed over the hard, feminine body against hers: tight breasts, jewel-hard nipples, and down the flat plane of her stomach to the softness of her sex. Appolonia moaned into her mouth and Cymone slid her fingers through the slick folds and into the drenched warmth there. She reached, finding the soft pad of flesh inside, the key to her lover's pleasure. She stroked the sensitive spot several times and soon, Cymone felt the telltale tremors of her lover's climax.

Before the last spasm, Appolonia's fingers delved between Cymone's legs. Cymone's thighs flew open as she rocked closer, sighing in pleasure at the sweet invasion. She clung to the lithe body countering hers as Appolonia expertly brought her to a second orgasm. Cymone's lips stilled. Her breath froze in her chest as she surrendered to mingling emotions of lust and love that swelled to overflowing.

Her hands moved up Appolonia's narrow back. Cymone held her head and sated herself of the other *gladiatrix's* mouth.

Whatever tomorrow would bring, she was ready. Appolonia had made her ready.

Cymone gazed into her lover's eyes and smiled. "I have denied myself for so long but I must tell you, I love you."

Appolonia's lush lips parted in wonder and surprise. "I love you, too. You must have known. Since the first time I saw you on the training ground, dressed in nothing but a loincloth and drenched in sweat." A smile stretched across her beautiful face.

Cymone thumbed back a strand of Appolonia's hair. "Whatever Athene has decided our fates to be tomorrow, I know I can face it. Because of you."

Cymone's heart twisted at the softness in Appolonia's dark eyes. And then, Appolonia moved lower to lave each breast before kissing a path downward where she buried her face in Cymone's *cunnus*.

Cymone captured the head between her legs, holding it in place as a warm tongue flicked over her slit and circled her clitoris. Lips closed on the aching bud, sucking with seductive intent. She dragged in a sharp breath, opening her thighs impossibly wider as a finger joined the tongue in the slow, thorough assault of Cymone's senses. What magical power did Appolonia possess to bring her to such bliss over and over again?

It was unlawful for *gladiatrices* to copulate with the men at the *ludus* or elsewhere, and while some of the warrior women defied the order, and others sought out the company of their fellow female fighters out of necessity, Cymone had always preferred a woman's touch.

Appolonia's touch.

A second finger joined the first and moments later, Cymone cried out as perfect pleasure crashed over her in rippling waves, eradicating all coherent thought.

Stillness descended in the wake of her orgasm, quieting her

nerves and her brain, leaving her to bask in the comfort of her lover's arms. For this one moment, she was no longer the *gladiatrix prima*, dominatrix of the arena. She was a woman who could be vulnerable and who could experience loving and being loved.

Cymone chased away the knowledge that this happiness was fleeting. For on the morrow, she would walk onto the sands a deadly warrior.

Appolonia closed her eyes as she strode toward the Gates of Life. Oiled and clad in nothing other than the *subligaculum*—a loincloth—she whispered a prayer to Athene. Here at the gates, silence ensued. Even the cheering of the crowds faded away until there was nothing but her thoughts to speak to her.

She knew not who she would face this day but honor demanded that she fight and fight well. In the arena, she ceased to be a slave. There, she shone as a *gladiatrix* ascending to the position of *prima*—a position she hoped never to take from her lover.

The great wooden gates began to lift and Appolonia spun each of her two swords in her fists. Adrenaline surged.

A roar arose from the crowd as she stepped into the light, anxious to see her opponent. But when she laid eyes on the warrior emerging from the opposite gate, her heart wrenched.

Cymone.

Appolonia gritted her teeth then straightened her shoulders and stepped forward toward her enemy.

GAME OVER

Elle

Jaysa's bathing suit was low on her hips, and as she dove into the pool it went a little lower than she would have desired. Marisa didn't mind; she actually enjoyed the view when Jaysa stepped out and adjusted her suit.

Marisa knew Jaysa from cheerleading. Jaysa was a new member, the only freshman allowed on the A squad in the past four years. Marisa, now a senior, had also made it as a freshman. Jaysa definitely didn't look like a freshman either. She had an incredible body for an eighteen-year-old, Marisa thought. Beautiful rack, like a C-cup maybe, high and round. Great legs, so nicely shaped, toned and long. Very smooth skin, a deep brown color, with a great stomach too. This girl had to do at least two hundred crunches a day—she had a perfect six-pack.

Marisa had a wonderful body too. She was the voluptuous, hourglass figure type. A little shorter than Jaysa's five seven, Marisa stood at five four. Everything about her seemed curved. Her hips, legs, ass, lips. Everything. While Jaysa was lithe, Marisa looked like she could bounce. Especially on her ass. She had natural red hair and greenish colored eyes, and while her coloring betrayed her Irish heritage, she had the body of a Latina. Marisa's looks greatly contrasted those of Native American Jaysa, with her dark skin and long straight black hair, and those deep, dark eyes that Marisa felt she could fall into sometimes.

Along with all the straight guys on campus, every new school year, Marisa checked out the freshman crop. She had had a freshman fling every year since she was a sophomore. Since she had work study in the registrar's office she had access to their files. That's how she found out that Jaysa has been a cheerleader in high school. So she approached Jaysa and suggested trying out for the A squad. What fun would it be if they weren't on the same squad? Marisa had a ready excuse for hanging out with the girl: she wanted to teach her the routines. It was also a good justification for physical intimacy.

Marisa loved handling Jaysa's body. Since the first day of the fall semester, when she had seen Jaysa walk across the quad in her low-rise, tight jeans and red tube top, Marisa's interest had been piqued. What a hottie! Marisa had been interested from that first view and so had a lot of other people, but Marisa happened to know that Jaysa had rejected every offer for a date made so far. Also, Jaysa had seemed very receptive when approached by Marisa, friendly even. Until then, Marisa had been turned on by Jaysa's apparent aloofness and unapproach-ability. It was one of her many asset's in Marisa's opinion. That bitch factor was such a turn-on for Marisa.

That's one of the reasons she liked the young'uns so much. Here was a smug little girl with these attitudes, who really didn't know anything at all. Not compared to a twenty-one-year-old like Marisa. The difference in maturity between a freshman and a senior was monumental. Marisa felt herself responsible for closing the gap a little.

She taught these girls a thing or two, usually a lot more. She took away some of that righteous attitude that a lot of them seemed to carry over from ruling their high schools. Marisa enjoyed the rule of instructor. And a lot of them needed instruction, since the majority of their experience consisted of fumbling around in backseats with awkward teenage boys. Marisa without fail chose virgins. It wasn't conscious, but every freshman she had chosen so far had been pure. Until they met Marisa.

Jaysa was something special, though, Marisa could feel it. She seemed wise, in spite of her years. She would give Marisa these looks that were so intense, Marisa would have to turn away. Maybe it was because she was Native American, Marisa thought. There might be some spiritual enlightenment Jaysa was privy to. Maybe it was that she was confident, *really* confident, not the pseudo-confidence other kids portrayed, which fell apart as soon as you got too close.

Whatever the reason, it set Jaysa apart from everyone else in Marisa's life. Marisa came close to orgasm a few times when they had sleepovers, from being too close and affectionate with each other. Jaysa had this manner of sleeping where she would completely entwine her body with yours. At least she did with Marisa. When Jaysa's legs were between hers, and Marisa could feel their breasts pressed against each other's, their nipples rubbing with their slight movement, these were the "almosts" for her. She would be on the verge of coming, and have to force herself to return to earth.

They had also developed the habit of giving each other quick pecks on the lips, which was torture for Marisa because all she wanted to do was slip her warm tongue into Jaysa's hot mouth.

By now she would have the freshman literally on her knees. She had lost control with this one, most definitely. Jaysa somehow had Marisa doubting herself—or at least her techniques. Marisa was getting tired of it, even though she was also kind of enjoying the prolonged courtship in a weird way. It was like an extremely long striptease, but Marisa wanted more. Jaysa had started undressing completely in front of her and it was driving Marisa almost to the brink. There were two or three times already that she had to literally restrain herself from pouncing on Jaysa's naked body. Especially when she would come out of the shower or the pool, soaking wet, and naked, walk around in front of Marisa. Marisa couldn't pounce; she couldn't react without a game plan.

One of those times she had offered Jaysa a massage, and the younger girl accepted, fully naked. Marisa really took her time, getting into every nook and crevice. Rubbing really near Jaysa's breasts, kneading her thighs and her ass. All with the excuse of their grueling workout. Jaysa seemed to really enjoy it, letting out a few moans during the session. She was extremely satiated afterward, lounging around like a cat, smiling. Then she offered Marisa a massage. When Marisa accepted and turned to lie on her stomach, Jaysa asked why she wasn't getting undressed. So, Marisa ended up receiving a massage from Jaysa fully naked too. Jaysa seemed to pay special attention to Marisa's ivory inner thighs, rubbing between Marisa's legs until she was sure Jaysa could tell how wet she was.

Oh, my god, Marisa had thought—*what a gift!* Jaysa's hands were amazingly strong, yet soft. They made Marisa feel she was someplace else—surrounded by beautiful naked women all touching her and each other. This was a fantasy Marisa had when she was masturbating. Lately, though, her thoughts turned to Jaysa's naked body pressed against hers, between her legs, the two of them grinding against each other. Or her face buried in Jaysa's full breasts, grabbing Jaysa's ass, sucking on those big, beautiful brown nipples. Gently tugging on them with her teeth, causing Jaysa to writhe, moan and gyrate against Marisa's pelvic area, rubbing against her clit. Yes, lately *this* was getting her off. Marisa was dying to immerse her fingers in Jaysa's wetness. To push inside her, to make her hips rock back and forth. To watch Jaysa's tantalizing body as she fucked her. When was this going to happen?

Marisa felt like she couldn't wait any longer. She felt like she was going to implode or worse yet, come when it wasn't appropriate, like during a nudie massage session. How would that appear to Jaysa? No, that would definitely not be cool at all, and Marisa certainly had to at least maintain the *image* of being cool. At least the image of coolness, because she certainly didn't feel cool around Jaysa whatsoever. In fact, it was the total opposite. She was nervous around Jaysa, flustered even. That was why she hadn't made a move yet. She would've been knee-deep in panties by now with any other freshman meat. It definitely wasn't for lack of desire. Marisa wanted Jaysa so bad; she almost constantly had her on the brain. The fantasies would get more elaborate and more frequent. Especially now that they were hanging out so often, every day after class and on weekends there was always one sleepover night at either of the girl's houses. Jaysa had even dropped this bomb the other day: "You're like my best friend now, Mar."

Oh, god, the last thing Marisa wanted to be was Jaysa's friend. Her lover, her instructor, sure, but not that…that word… *friend.* Even though that was sometimes a safe precursor for the girls to "experiment." But when would that be?

Marisa had come close to touching Jaysa's breast the other day when they had tongue-kissed. Marisa had been able to taste

Jaysa's sweet mouth when they had been talking about their past sexual experiences. Jaysa said she had an ex-boyfriend who kissed like a snake, and when words failed to describe his lack of skill, Jaysa decided to put on a physical demonstration. Which went from being a sort of funny, serpentine kiss to a real passionate, deep tongue-kiss that left them both panting and moist. Marisa continued that kiss by offering to demonstrate how *good* one of her exes used to kiss. This led to a ten-minute makeout session between Jaysa and Marisa. After, Jaysa asked how Marisa could've broken up with someone who kissed so well. Marisa reveled in the compliment, completely reciprocating it by telling Jaysa that it takes two people to kiss well. Then Jaysa asked Marisa if she minded kissing her. Marisa answered that it was the opposite; she actually enjoyed it. When she also assured Jaysa that there was nothing wrong with them kissing, Jaysa smiled at the comment. Then she told Marisa good night and nestled into Marisa's body the way she did when they slept together. Marisa had a difficult time falling asleep that evening. She was so stimulated and also agonizing over what that smile had meant. And why the apparent brush-off? Didn't Jaysa feel anything? Didn't Marisa excite her? Could she have misjudged this one so badly?

The next day gave her the answer: Jaysa confronted Marisa. She asked why Marisa hadn't made a move. To say Marisa was in shock would be an understatement. She must've stared at Jaysa for a full minute before responding. How to answer her? Marisa's agonizing last night was nothing compared to this fear, personified by the bold freshman standing in front of her demanding to know why Marisa hadn't done what she so wanted to do. "I know you want me. So why haven't you made a move?" Jaysa had a way with words, with everything really. A hundred responses ran through Marisa's mind, from denial to a physical answer. She finally settled on the truth. No games for once. "Because you have me all mixed up. I don't know how to approach you. It's the only time this has happened to me. I think it's because you're so self-possessed." Jaysa laughed. She then told Marisa that she had been waiting for her to do something since the first time they had hung out. "See, that's what I get for playing along. I don't do games. But I thought you wanted that... I thought you wanted to be the aggressor. So I was waiting for you to do something...but you never did. Not really, anyway. I've had girlfriends before, you know? I'm completely into girls, always have been. I don't have a problem with it."

This confrontation completely reaffirmed all the admiration Marisa had for Jaysa. This girl was something else, for real. "Well, you kind of do something weird to me. I've never really felt like this about anybody. You make me feel self-conscious," Marisa responded honestly. She felt a relief *and* a panic from this encounter. So Jaysa was into her; that was good news. She was also very dominant apparently, which Marisa wasn't sure about. She was aroused though, she had to admit, by Jaysa's ballsiness. The way Jaysa was upfront about her sexuality and her desires was very refreshing. Marisa played games because everyone else did and she had to assure her own safety. She didn't want to put herself out there, be completely vulnerable. Apparently Jaysa had no qualms about being vulnerable, which made Marisa want her even more.

Jaysa grabbed her hands, "So, are you ready to stop playing?" Jaysa was standing in front of her in cutoff jean shorts and a wife-beater with no bra. Marisa could practically taste Jaysa's nipples through the tank top. Why was she so nervous? Maybe it was because she wasn't in control of this situation the way she had been with all the other girls. Or maybe because Jaysa had something to compare her to. Marisa wasn't sure, and she didn't want to know, either. She just wanted to enjoy the time with Jaysa. Also, this was her last year with Jaysa: in June she was graduating. So she just nodded. Jaysa pulled her into the bedroom from where they were standing on the veranda. Finally Marisa was going to get what she had been pining after for so long.

That night Marisa had the best sex she ever had. Jaysa was a considerate and experienced lover. Marisa had so many orgasms she lost count. Jaysa really knew how to pleasure a woman, in every way. They spent what seemed like eight hours exploring each other's body. Jaysa told Marisa that the experience was "mind-blowing." They took two showers together during the long night. The sex in the shower was so hot that Marisa almost came just looking at Jaysa's glistening breasts and thighs.

Jaysa liked to fuck hard and Marisa had no problem with that. She would pound her fingers into Marisa furiously, making her come dozens of times. She also used a strap-on dildo, which Marisa had never experienced before. It was a little painful, but as Jaysa said, "It's hard to find pleasure without any pain." Marisa got used to it quick. Jaysa also had a habit of biting— no, more like chewing—on Marisa's nipples. This drove Marisa crazy, because no girl had ever done that to her before and it felt so good. After such an amazing experience, there was no way either of them wanted to lose touch after the school year ended. Marisa was going to get a job in the real world and Jaysa would still have three more years of college. They planned to continue their relationship during summers and holidays, with Jaysa maybe moving to the city after graduation so they would be closer to each other. Regardless of what might happen in the future, this experience with Jaysa had changed Marisa forever.

Who says you don't learn anything senior year?

ABOUT THE AUTHORS

CHEYENNE BLUE isn't sure if she runs so she can eat, or if she eats so she can run. Her erotica has appeared in many anthologies, including *Best Women's Erotica*, *Mammoth Best New Erotica*, *Best Lesbian Erotica* and *Best Lesbian Romance*. She currently lives in Queensland, Australia. Visit her website at cheyenneblue.com.

KIKI DELOVELY is a queer femme performer/writer whose work has appeared in *Best Lesbian Erotica 2011*, *Salacious* magazine, *Gotta Have It: 69 Stories of Sudden Sex* and *Take Me There: Transgender and Genderqueer Erotica*. Kiki's greatest passions include artichokes, words, alternative baking, and taking on research for her writing.

DELILAH DEVLIN is a prolific and award-winning author of erotica and erotic romance with a rapidly expanding reputation for writing deliciously edgy stories with complex characters. She has published over ninety erotic stories in multiple subgenres with Avon, Cleis Press, Kensington, Atria/Strebor, Ellora's Cave, Samhain Publishing and Berkley.

ELLE is just elle.

SHANNA GERMAIN doesn't play tennis, but she can serve a volleyball like you wouldn't believe. Her work has appeared in places like *Best American Erotica, Best Gay Romance, Best Erotic Romance, Best Lesbian Erotica* and *Best Lesbian Romance*. Visit her naughty side of the net at *shannagermain.com.*

SACCHI GREEN's stories have appeared in a hip-high stack of publications with erotically inspirational covers, and she's also edited or coedited eight erotica anthologies, including *Girl Crazy, Lesbian Cowboys* (winner of the 2010 Lambda Literary Award for lesbian erotica,) *Lesbian Lust, Lesbian Cops* and *Girl Fever,* all from Cleis Press.

Editor of *Carnal Machines, Spank, The Sweetest Kiss* and the Lammy Finalist, *Where the Girls Are,* find **D. L. KING's** stories in *Best Lesbian Erotica, Best Women's Erotica, Girl Crazy* and *Broadly Bound,* among others. She's published two novels and edits the review site Erotica Revealed. Find her at dlkingerotica.com.

JT LANGDON is the Taoist, vegetarian and lover of chocolate responsible for such erotic novels as the *Lady Davenport's Slave* trilogy, *She-Devils* and *The Sisters of Omega-Pi.* For more of JT's incessant ramblings, including poetry and short fiction, be sure to visit jtlangdon.com.

GINA MARIE lives, writes and dreams in the Pacific Northwest. She has authored erotic fiction for Clean Sheets, Oysters & Chocolate, *Lucrezia Magazine*, Sacchi Green's *Where the Girls Are* and her own e-anthology, *Opening Eden*. She is also a poet and photographer. Check out her naughty blog at aphrodites-table.blogspot.com.

SOMMER MARSDEN is the wine-swigging, dachshund owning, wannabe runner author of *Learning to Drown, We Kill Dead Things, Hard Lessons* and *Wanderlust*. She's the editor of *Gritty: Rough Erotic Fiction, Dirtyville, Kinkyville* and *Coupling: Filthy Erotica for Couples*. She's perpetually up to no good on her blog Unapologetic Fiction at sommermarsden.blogspot.com.

SINCLAIR SEXSMITH (mrsexsmith.com) runs the award-winning project *Sugarbutch Chronicles*. Her work appears in *Best Lesbian Erotica, Persistence: All Ways Butch and Femme* and *Take Me There: Transgender and Genderqueer Erotica*, and she edited Cleis's *Say Please: Lesbian BDSM Erotica*. Mr. Sexsmith writes, teaches and performs.

PAISLEY SMITH (Paisley-Smith.com) is a full-time freelance writer and can usually be found in front of her computer either writing, chatting, promoting or plotting. She attended college in the Deep South where she obtained a slew of totally useless degrees and developed an unrelenting sense of humor.

In ANNA WATSON's household, everything came to a halt as she, her butch husband and their two boys watched every thrilling moment of the Women's World Cup. Aren't you glad Abby Wambach finally cut her hair? Anna has stories in *Best*

Lesbian Erotica 12, Best Lesbian Romance 12, Take Me There and *The Harder She Comes.*

ALLISON WONDERLAND (aisforallison.blogspot.com) is one L of a girl. Her lesbian literature appears in *Bound by Lust, Best Lesbian Erotica 2010, Alison's Wonderland, Gertrude, Milk and Honey, Undressed Erotica* and *Passionate Hearts.* In addition to Sapphic storytelling, Allison's indulgences include cotton candy, kitten heels, and Old Hollywood glamour.

Erotica author **BETH WYLDE** writes what she likes to read, which includes a little bit of everything. Her muse is an equal opportunity plot bunny that believes everyone, no matter their kink, color, gender or orientation is entitled to love, acceptance and scalding HOT sex! Find Beth at bethwylde.com.

ABOUT
THE EDITOR

ILY GOYANES is a Cuban-American, a political moderate, an expert billiards player, a liger and somewhat of a Zelig, but above all else she is a seeker of knowledge. She lives in Miami, Florida with her children, dogs, cat and assorted hangers on. Goyanes is commonly known as the Fuming Foodie—a controversial, yet amusing persona she has cultivated via her weekly column of the same name. In addition to her food column, she also writes about film, theater, music and popular culture for the *Miami New Times* (Village Voice Media), is a published erotic fiction writer, and is the editor-in-chief of Arketipo 187 Magazine (arketipo187.com), a digital magazine that covers news, culture, and lifestyle. Ampersand Editions (ampersandeditions.com), her publishing house, keeps her busy when she isn't writing. For more information, to cuss at and/or praise her or to invite her to a game of pool or a plate of Mexican food, she encourages you (strongly) to email her at ily.goyanes@gmail.com.